HOLIDAY WITH HADES

MYSTICAL MIDLIFE IN MAINE BOOK 4

BRENDA TRIM

Copyright © December 2021 by Brenda Trim
Editor: Chris Cain
Cover Art by Fiona Jayde

* * *

This book is a work of fiction. The names, characters, places, and incidents are products of the writers' imagination or have been used fictitiously and are not to be construed as real. Any resemblance to persons, living or dead, actual events, locales or organizations is entirely coincidental.

WARNING: The unauthorized reproduction of this work is illegal. Criminal copyright infringement is investigated by the FBI and is punishable by up to 5 years in federal prison and a fine of $250,000.

All rights reserved. With the exception of quotes used in reviews, this book may not be reproduced or used in whole or in part by any means existing without written permission from the authors.

❦ Created with Vellum

This book is for my family. They're a little bit crazy. Extremely loud. And always full of love. Thanks for all the holiday memories. Love you to the moon and back!

CHAPTER 1

"Are you kidding me? I can't imagine Hattie being shy like that. She always spoke her mind without apology." I laughed as Tarja told us stories about a fifteen-year-old Hattie trying to tell the boy she liked that she wanted to date him.

I heard the scratchy coughing laugh of my familiar fill my head. *"Hattie was young and insecure once, despite being the heir to the Pleaides witch power. Back then, she was gangly and awkward. And completely in love with James. She thought the sun and moon hung in that warlock's brown eyes."*

Mythia hovered near the Christmas tree with a garland strand in her hand. She paused in winding it around the branches. "I remember when she invited James over to the house to study. She cast a spell to make her boobs bigger, and they ended up so big the buttons on her shirt popped open. Her mother was mortified that she flashed James. Of course, he didn't mind it at all."

My son laughed. "I bet he didn't. What happened? Did they date and eventually get married?" My heart ached at his question. He didn't know Hattie never married. And, he had no idea she was brutally attacked and rendered barren.

Tarja shook her head from side to side before she batted a glass ball toward the tree. *"Hattie never dated James and never married. She threw herself into creating a corporation that would be able to support magical kind. She had a dream of giving witches and warlocks a safe place to work where they didn't have to fear losing control of their magic."* I was distracted by what Tarja was saying. She used her familiar powers to make the glass decoration float before settling on one of the branches.

"I wish I had that kind of control over my magic," I blurted. My familiar's abilities always made me feel like an imposter. It didn't help that I wasn't born to cast spells and use magic. I was a mundane human until six months ago.

Nana snorted. "Tarja's had centuries to perfect her craft where you've only been at it for a few months. You shouldn't be so hard on yourself. You've accomplished far more than I expected this soon."

My mom inclined her head. "Nana is right, sweetie. Stop beating yourself up and expecting so much."

I sighed and unplugged the strand of white lights. My favorite part of the holidays was decorating the tree and enjoying the bulbs that twinkled in the branches. "I know what you both are saying is true, but I can't help but feel like there's something wrong with me. I mean, look at Stella. She doesn't have nearly as many issues as I do with my casting and potion-making. It comes so easy for her."

Tarja placed a paw on my leg and looked at me with solemn eyes. *"Ordinary witches aren't the best people to judge your performance against. They wield a fraction of the energy coursing through your body. While they're channeling the equivalent of a blow torch, you're funneling a volcano. That takes time and practice to master. Hattie blew up half of this house when she was learning. It had to be rebuilt after her first lessons."*

My eyes widened, and my chest warmed. I'd become far closer than I ever could have imagined to my familiar over the past six months. I hardly remembered how I used to think Tarja was a spoiled feline and Hattie a crazy cat lady. "I'll have to keep that in mind. I love this house and would hate to blow it up."

"I don't know. I could use a bigger closet," Nana said as she handed my mom the ornament with my handprint that I made in elementary school.

I snorted and shook my head. "You don't need anything else. You use my closet and Hattie's clothes more than you do your own."

Jean-Marc chuckled. "Your closet is bigger than three of my dorm rooms, Nana. Mom's right. You have plenty of room in there. By the way, mom. Is your boyfriend coming over to help decorate?"

My heart skipped several beats, and my body lit on fire at the mere mention of Aidoneus. "I wouldn't call him my boyfriend, Jean-Marc. And, I didn't invite him over."

One of my son's eyebrows lifts to his hairline. "Well, then what do you consider him? You're obviously in a relationship. There was no mistaking how much he liked you when I was here a couple months ago. And, I know you two have only gotten closer since I returned to school."

I scowled at my oldest child. I didn't want to think about this at the moment. Let alone defend it to him. Their father burned me too badly for me to trust easily. I wanted to take things slow with Aidon. "I'm not entirely sure what we are. We like each other, and he helps when things go sideways with the magical beings in town. We also watch over the Hellmouth together. Maybe it's that bond we share that makes you think we are so close."

Nina picked up the popcorn strand she just finished and draped one corner on the tree. "It's not the Hellmouth, mom.

And it isn't the demons or other crises that have made you two close. From the first day you met him, there has been some connection between the two of you."

Nana nodded and gestured with her hands. The crystal icicle she held glinted like a weapon from the strands hanging on the tree in the low lighting. "Nina is right, Pheeb. I never have believed in love at first sight or soul mates, but the way he looks at you had me rethinking my position on the topic. There's no way you can deny what the two of you share."

My cheeks heated as I stood behind the Douglas fir while gathering my composure. A secret part of me wanted to believe what they were saying to me. Losing Aidon like I did Miles wouldn't be something I got over easily.

My ex-husband, Miles, was a selfish prick and always had been. I was too infatuated to see him clearly when I was younger, though. As a twenty-something young woman in college, I thought he hung the stars and moon. When I finished my nursing program, he was in medical school, studying to be a cardiothoracic surgeon. Miles seemed like the perfect guy back then.

Now, I was dating an honest to goodness god that thought I was gorgeous, intelligent, and talented. And he is considerate in bed, giving me orgasm after orgasm. There was no question he was better than my ex.

Good thing you aren't that young, stupid woman anymore. You might let this god slip through your fingers while pursuing a man that couldn't be bothered to see to your pleasure for over a decade.

I attached the next strand of lights and stepped out from behind the tree. "I do not deny anything, Nana. But he is a god with thousands of years of experience. I'm hardly more than a mundie." I left out the part about how worried I was that I wouldn't be able to hold his interest for long.

My mother shrugged her shoulders. "You're making

Nana's point for her, sweetheart. Aidon has had countless experiences and likely been with more women than I can fathom. And yet, he's completely besotted with you. He wouldn't be if you were just an ordinary woman. You're a rare gem, Phoebe. One he's lucky to know."

I choked out a laugh. Her words hit home. She was absolutely right about everything she said, but embracing that belief was dangerous. "Let's talk about something else. How has your magic been, Jean-Marc?"

My son shot me a look that said he was going to protest, but it quickly vanished. Likely because he could see how much I did not want to discuss this topic anymore. "It's been wonky. I can't predict when it's going to act up. I set my philosophy professor's textbook on fire a few weeks ago and met a witch in my class when I did. Emlyn's amazing, mom. She took me to the ley lines and taught me how to draw from the energy surrounding us. That helped stabilize me."

Nina's eyes went wide, and she smirked at her brother. Uh oh. "Oooo. You love her, don't you? Have you kissed her yet? I bet she spends more nights in your dorm room than in her own. Leave it to you to fall for the first witch you meet."

Jean-Marc smacked Nina's shoulder. "Shut up, turd. You're just jealous because you don't have any witch or warlock friends."

Nina thrust her hands onto her hips and growled at her brother. "I do too. Mom runs the coven in Camden, idiot. I have more witch and warlock friends than you can imagine. Plus, I'm friends with pixies, shifters, and vampires."

That got my attention. "Vampires? Since when have you made a vampire friend, young lady?"

Nina rolled her eyes and waved a hand through the air. "I met him at school, mom. Keir was born a vampire and doesn't feed on people. His parents get blood from the blood banks."

I nudged Tarja with my toes. *"Do I need to be worried a vampire attends school with Nina? Aren't they bloodthirsty demons?"*

My familiar didn't look at me as she responded. *"There are vampires that refuse to follow decorum and use caution, but most take steps to keep their existence hidden. The dangerous clans are ruthless. I can't see them sending their kids to school. For the most part, they aren't blood-thirsty creatures. In fact, the majority are like any paranormal and would never hurt another in pursuit of blood. Don't judge Keir before you meet him."*

"I won't. Thank you." I shifted my focus to Jean-Marc. "So, Emlyn, huh? What's she like?" I didn't trust many witches outside my immediate circle after my experience with Myrna.

Jean-Marc's cheeks pinkened, and he averted his gaze and started looking through our box of ornaments. "She's super smart. And a great witch. She's a natural at casting balls of light. She doesn't even seem to think about it. She's funny, too. It's easy to hang with her. We have no awkward moments, and she seems to understand what I feel before I do, so she's got a lot of insight."

My little guy was definitely falling for this witch. It was evident in the way he lit up when he talked about her. I smiled and continued with the lights. "Emlyn sounds wonderful. I can't wait to meet her."

"Does she know mom's the new Pleiades?" Nina asked as she continued grabbing decorations from the boxes.

I walked over and put the Santas back. The magical world celebrated Yule and winter solstice, not Christmas. And I was determined to have a mix of traditions to form our own without offending my new friends or family.

"Let's leave the Santas out of the festivities this year. They don't fit Yule, and we are developing a new path for the holidays this year." Nina nodded her head, and I focused on the question she'd asked her brother. "Have you told her about me?"

Jean-Marc lowered his eyes and chewed his lower lip. "I haven't said anything to her. I didn't know what to say. You've had enough people attacking you, and while I think she's great, she might have a crazy mom or something. The last thing I want is to cause more problems for you, mom."

Tears sprang to my eyes, and I wrapped my son in a hug. "I'm not sure if that's necessary, but thank you for thinking of me." I released him. "What do you think, Tarja?"

My familiar stretched her back. *"Few witches pose a threat to you. Most will worship the ground you walk on. We will know if her family is Tainted when we meet her. Even if her parents have Turned, they will imprint her as their daughter that we can detect. Although, chances are good her parents work for you. Thousands of witches and warlocks do."*

Hearing about the company I inherited made me feel guilty. I'd been to the offices in Camden but haven't traveled to others yet, and I needed to. Lilith had been hounding me to make plans to meet the other site managers and see production at the various plants throughout the globe.

A knock at the door interrupted my response. "I'll get it." I'd bet it was Stella. Her husband worked tonight, and she was no doubt bored. Or afraid to be home with her kids. She'd told her family she was a witch, and they'd been stand-offish with her ever since.

My resident ghoul passed me carrying a tray of hot cocoas and a slab of ribs. I hope she didn't get barbeque sauce in the chocolate concoction like she did last time. Seeing her sparked my guilt over not having the answers for how to give her a soul. It was the only way to protect her from future possession. She hadn't left the house in longer than I cared to admit. Not that I blamed her.

She had no soul inhabiting her body as a ghoul, so it was

like chumming the ocean on a shark expedition. Unholy creatures flocked to her like flies to shit. The stories of zombies had to have originated from possessed ghouls. Beings from the Underworld loved death and destruction, and inside, a being like Selene could devour an entire town in a week.

A smile spread across my face the second I opened the door and laid eyes on the guy darkening my doorstep. "Aidon! What are you doing here? Please tell me there aren't demons we have to go hunt down. Selene just made hot cocoa, and we're decorating the house."

Aidoneus smirked and sauntered into the house as he reached for me. His hands landed on my hips, and his body heat obliterated the cold air seeping inside the open front door. I barely noticed when he kicked the panel closed because his mouth descended on mine and stole my ability to think straight.

My world narrowed down to the god embracing me and how he was kissing me senseless. His lips were ravenous, and his hands roamed over my backside before squeezing. I was struck with the urge to rip our clothes off and take him right then and there.

The sound of a throat clearing brought me back to Earth with a crash. The sound was more profound than anyone living in the house, which told me it was my son. I broke away from Aidon's mouth with my face heating with embarrassment at being caught.

Jean-Marc had a knowing smirk on his face. "Are you certain he's not your boyfriend, mom? I don't go around kissing friends or acquaintances."

I rolled my eyes and headed into the living room. "I'm not sure what Aidon and I are. We have no need to put a label on it. I think we're both beyond needing anything so trivial."

Aidoneus caught up with me and wrapped an arm around

my waist, tugging me closer to him as I walked. The action nearly made me fall into him before I caught my balance. "My father would disagree with you, Queenie. He's coming here to meet the witch that stole my heart and claims to be my mate."

I stop, making him bump into my shoulder as I whirl around and face him. "What did you just say?"

"He said his dad is coming to meet you, Phoebe. You might want to get a CT scan before he arrives to ensure you aren't suffering from brain damage. You did take several hits to the skull a couple months ago," Nana shared, trying to be helpful.

Aidoneus cupped my cheek. "He's upset I'm not in his realm anymore, and my mother insisted on seeing me for the holidays. So he decided he'd use the trip as an opportunity to meet the woman that captured my heart."

My heart was racing so fast I thought I was going to pass out. I had to bend over and brace myself on my knees. My breath got caught in my throat. A fine sheen of sweat covered my entire body a second later as my hormones dropped from the high of a few minutes ago.

A hand rubbed up and down my back. I turned my head to look up at Aidon. He gave me a reassuring smile. Too bad it did nothing to abate my terror. "There's no reason to panic, Pheebs. He's going to love you. Well, I know my mom will like you for sure. Dad is another story altogether. He thinks I'm making the same mistakes he did when he mated my mother. He hates being away from her half of the year, but that was the only deal her mother was willing to make at the time."

Jean-Marc stepped forward. "Is he going to try and make my mom live in the Underworld half the time? She can't leave Earth."

I stood up straight and grabbed my son's hand. "I'm not

going anywhere as exotic as another realm, peanut. And, I don't think meeting your dad is a good idea. I'm a middle-aged woman with an attitude and a sarcastic mouth. He already blames me for you living here. We don't need to add rocket fuel to the fire."

My mother put her hands on her hips, twinkle lights dangling from one hand. "Phoebe Alicia Dieudonne`. You will not talk negatively about yourself. I made you from scratch and did a damn good job if I do say so myself. You're beautiful, intelligent, caring, and as loyal as they come. Hades would be lucky if you decided to mate his son. And I'll tell him that when I meet him."

Tears sprang to my eyes, and I had to choke back the emotion burning in my throat. I was on a freaking roller coaster with no restraints and swore I was going to fly off any second. "I don't think you need to tell the God Hades anything, mom. I like you in one piece. But I needed that reminder. I am who I am, and I won't apologize for that. It took me months to start loving myself after Miles, and I'm not going to let anyone, even a god make me feel bad about what I look like or who I am. That being said, are you sure meeting him is a good idea?"

"My dad's bark is worse than his bite. He won't do anything knowing how much you mean to me. I'm more worried about him scaring you into bailing on us before we reach our full potential," Aidoneus admitted.

Nina set her cocoa down and looked from Aidon to me. "He can't break you guys up. The two of you are already tied together for eternity or something like that because of the Hellmouth, right? I'd be more worried he wants grandkids if I were you, mom." I gaped at my daughter. I never considered that.

"This is what's called dating, mom. Just so you're aware. Also, meeting the parents is a serious step," Jean-Marc added.

"Shut up, you two. You know if Aidon and I do get mated, then Hades is your step-grandfather." I laughed when Nina paled, and Jean-Marc vacillated between shaking and smiling. My son couldn't decide if that was cool or terrifying. I'd go with the latter if I were him.

Aidon laughed with me and shook his head. "No one needs to be afraid. My father is going to love everyone."

Famous last words, I thought. "When is he coming?"

"Winter solstice," Aidon replied.

My heart dropped like a stone. "That's only a few days away. Oh my God. This house isn't ready for a god." I would have preferred to have the floors redone and get new furniture.

I never bothered to redo things after Hattie died. Her taste was old-fashioned for me, but doing anything different was a waste of money. Now I had to see what I could get accomplished before his arrival. The holidays were suddenly more stressful than when I was married to Miles. He insisted on perfection for his mother and father.

CHAPTER 2

I shoved the brown leather sofa back and ran the vacuum on the area rug in the middle of the living room. Is that a stain? I crouched and bent close to inspect the area rug Nana insisted on bringing from home. I was more than happy to accommodate her and my mom when they moved into Hattie's house with me, but now I questioned my sanity.

I had a god coming over for the holidays, and mom and Nana didn't have the nicest of stuff. It was homey, and I loved it, but it was not fit for Hades. I should have kept the furniture in the house instead of giving it to Lilith's daughter to furnish her new home. I could have stored it and brought it back in while Hades visited.

I grabbed the rag off the coffee table along with the bottle of cleaner and sprayed the stain. *The* God of the Underworld is going to visit *my* house. What do you serve a god like Hades? Somehow, I doubt he'll like lobster rolls and chowder.

When I consider the meal my family has eaten for decades at Christmas, and I try to picture Hades sitting at the table, my mind refuses to accept the ridiculous image of an eight-foot-tall version of Aidoneus joining us.

Certain I got the stain out, I stop scrubbing the carpet and sigh when I can still see the outline of it. I can't do much more without destroying the fibers of the rug. After setting the rag and cleaner down, I got up and resumed the vacuuming while my brain tried to create another plan for dinner.

Not that I was hungry in the least. My stomach was a knot, and bile filled the back of my throat while my mind raced faster than my heart. Usually, I wouldn't give a second thought to meeting my boyfriend's parents, but Hades wasn't your average father. He could smite me in the blink of an eye.

Mythia's tiny pixie form hovered in front of my face. Her iridescent wings fluttered rapidly, and her arms waved in front of my face. "There is no need for you to do this cleaning, Phoebe. It's my job, and I will do it. Unless you're unhappy with how I keep the house."

I stopped pushing the machine and turned it off. I never stopped to consider how my best pixie friend would take my actions. "I couldn't be happier with how you take care of things here and keep the house running. You are doing a better job than I ever could. It's nothing you did or didn't do."

Nina walked through the room with a soda in her hand. "Yeah, mom cleans when she's nervous about someone visiting. Actually, she becomes a maniac anytime we have people over. Whether it's a party or just a few friends. I've always considered it her OCD coming out to play."

I rolled my eyes. "I'm not that bad. And, it isn't OCD. It's called wanting to make sure everything is perfect when people see our house."

Nana snorted from her perch in the recliner. "Perfect is a ridiculous notion. There is nothing wrong with the house. Or you, for that matter. In fact, I would say both are absolutely flawless. I would have thought you'd gotten to the point where you're comfortable with yourself and your house the way it is. If someone looks down their nose at you and your surroundings, they don't deserve your consideration. Our house isn't a magazine. We live in it, and it should look like we do."

My mind immediately jumped to the plethora of flaws I had. I opened my mouth to list them for my grandmother, then closed it. She was right. I took pride in myself and my home, even before inheriting Hattie's mansion. I'd stopped caring what other people's idea of perfection was months ago.

"I'd normally agree with you, Nana. But *Hades, the God of the Underworld, is coming for a visit*. We can't feed him lobster rolls before we open matching pajamas and sit in front of the tree for a family picture."

Mythia's face split into a wide smile. "Oh! That sounds like a great tradition. I wish my family had something that united us like that."

I returned her smile. "We do, Thia. I've got my mom looking for a seamstress to create your pajamas."

Glitter fell from Mythia's body as her wings fluttered faster, and she started glowing. "I'm included? I've never been included before."

"Of course, you're included. So is Selene. You're both part of the family," I assure her.

"So is Aidoneus and Hades, Phoebe. You're trying too hard to impress him when you should just be yourself. He will respect you for your strength and determination. Not your fancy furniture and stain-free rug. That stain was made when you brought the kids home for the holidays when Nina was seven. She spilled her fruit punch and tried to hide it from us because she was afraid Santa wouldn't bring her presents," Nana told me.

I didn't remember that. It sounded like something Nina would do. What shocked me was that I didn't notice it at the time and clean the stain. "You never told me."

Nana shook her head with a slight smile on her face. "No. I told Nina Santa would only deny her toys if she didn't take responsibility for what she'd done and clean it up. She did her best, and I couldn't go behind her and make her feel like she wasn't good enough. There's nothing worse than growing up feeling as if you can't ever do it right. It's just a rug. Not worth the negative impact on her confidence." That was precisely what I had done with Mythia. I'd inadvertently undermined her confidence by going on a cleaning rampage throughout the house.

Nana was a wise woman. One I hadn't taken advantage of nearly often enough. "Clearly, I haven't listened to you often enough. How do I host Hades without developing an ulcer, refurbishing the entire house after cleaning it from top to bottom? I feel the need to point out I will be asking Thia to go after me with her expertise to really make the place shine."

Nana sipped the coffee in her travel mug before setting it on the end table next to her. "It always shines, sweetheart. The only thing you need to do for Hades is give him a gift. A token of your appreciation for fathering the man you love. And stop giving him more power over your thoughts and actions. You are enough just as you are, Phoebe. Never doubt that."

I smiled at Nana and prayed her words sunk into my addled brain. Meeting Hades took me back a couple decades and made me doubt *everything*. I wasn't a twenty-something-year-old woman anymore. Back then, I worried about how every article of clothing looked on me and spent an hour each day fussing over my makeup and hair. Hours I should have spent studying for classes.

"What do you get a god?" I started pacing the room as I

focused on the one piece of advice I could act on right now. I had to do something, or the anxiety would get the better of me.

Mythia picked up the feather duster she preferred to use and started running it over the knickknacks that Nana and my mom added to the shelves when they moved in. I had the few items I left my marriage with. My kids' bronzed shoes and my favorite pictures of us.

"You should make him something he cannot buy anywhere else. It will show him your skill and give him a priceless heirloom." My brows furrowed. The tiny pixie had some great advice at times, and it always shocked me. This was one such instance.

"That's a great idea. I keep thinking that gods can literally conjure anything they could ever desire. What could I possibly give him? Making him something is really my only option." I needed to get some assistance with this task to make sure it turned out great.

Selene pushed off from the doorjamb leading into the kitchen. "You could always make him a grandchild. That's something I bet he would love to get. It's something he has never received in all of his existence, right?"

My heart hammered in my chest, and sweat rolled down my spine while I shuddered. I was too old to have kids now. "I have no idea if he has grandchildren or would even want them. Aidon never mentioned siblings, but I imagine he has plenty. What matters is that it is not happening. I'm forty-three years old. Beyond my childbearing years."

My mom poked her head in from the kitchen. "You are at the end of your childbearing years, but not beyond them, Phoebe. I noticed you never said you didn't want more kids. If that's the case, you will want to think about that and act fast. You aren't getting any younger."

"Actually, you are physically younger than your chronological

age. The magic you inherited reversed some of the natural damage from aging. I told you the most powerful witches live longer than mundies. The magic acts to preserve your fragile body. And, I suspect the bond you formed with Aidon had further changed you."

I glanced around, looking for the tabby coat of my cat familiar but didn't find her. I released a growl. She was always present and in the back of my mind and had a habit of interjecting herself in conversations. Usually, I appreciated her presence and information. Today not so much.

A glance at my mom and Nana told me she shared that with me alone. I knew Tarja was right. The magic had changed Nana and my mom, too. Nana moved faster and had more energy than she did a few months ago. I was grateful for her renewed vigor. It meant I would have more time with her.

"That is a discussion for never. Right now, I need help from Thicket with my gift. Can you get him, Thia?" I asked the pixie.

Mythia paused from her perch on the top shelf and nodded. "I'll go grab him and be right back. Should I send him down to your workroom?"

"Yes, please. Thank you. Are you going to join me, Nana? How about you, mom? Selene?" I asked as I headed for the kitchen and the door to the basement next to the pantry.

Selene shrugged her shoulders. "I'd love to join you if it won't bother you." Ever since her possession, the ghoul stayed close to my side when I was in the house. When I was gone, she stuck to my mother's side.

"The more, the merrier. I could use the moral support." I patted the ghoul on the shoulder as I passed by her.

Nina removed her head from the fridge and looked over at us. "What are you guys up to?"

"Going down to the workroom to watch your mom make Hades a Yule gift. You should join us." My mother and Nina had a close relationship. Something I didn't have with Nana until I returned home this past year.

After the mess of my divorce from Miles, I worried my kids would be hurt by not having their father in their lives as much as they were used to. Nina was better off because my mom doted on her and attended her activities, where her father never did.

Nina turned back to the open cooler, pulled out a Tupperware of strawberries, and then shut the door. "What are you going to make, mom? Oh! You should make him a protection charm. You're good at those now." She fingered the fifth dragonfly hanging from her neck. This one was a work of art. It had taken me weeks to work the silver into the delicate image.

I laughed as I flipped on the switch at the top of the basement stairs. "I'm not making jewelry for a God. Hades has no need for my paltry protection spell, anyway."

Nina took a seat on one of the stools next to the empty worktable. Magic hummed from the worn wooden surface. "Then get him tickets to Greenland or Nova Scotia. He has to be tired of the hot weather in Hell, right?"

The breath left me on a chuckle as I was bent over, grabbing the silver I would need from the bottom drawer of a cabinet. "From what Aidon has talked about, the Underworld is not like our myths about Hell. Besides, if Hades wanted to go someplace cold, he could simply teleport himself there."

"Good point," Nina agreed. "You could always make a shield for him. It's not jewelry. It's manly, or whatever, and he can hang it on his wall if he wants. Plus, it will be useful to him."

Thicket flew down the stairs at that moment. "Hello, Phoebe. We're making a shield today? All Mythia said was you needed my help with a gift for Hades. Is she talking about the God of the Underworld?"

"Hello, Thicket. Thanks for coming. I wasn't sure exactly what to make, but I liked Nina's idea for a shield. And yes. It will be for Hades, Aidoneus's father."

Thicket's hands shook as he hovered close to the recliner Nana was lowering herself into. "A shield sounds nice." The tiny pixie's voice was high-pitched like I'd expected the first time I saw him rather than the deep bass of a moment ago.

I extended a hand to him. "You are the most talented silversmith on the planet. Hades will be lucky to receive something you helped build."

Thicket's chest puffed up, and his pink cheeks spread into a grin. "We could make him a dagger to go with the sword, too. An enchanted pixie blade is almost as strong as what Hephaestus can make."

"Now, that is something I'm certain he will appreciate. With another god, Hades has to bargain and owes favors to procure any item, knowledge, or assistance," my mom interjected.

I started heating the silver with my magic like Thicket taught me. "How do you know all that, mom?"

Her cheeks turned pink as she shrugged her shoulders. "Books Aidoneus gave me. I asked him for information on his family so I could understand what you were joining ranks with."

The doorbell rang, interrupting my reply. Selene jumped from her position next to Nana on the floor. "I'll get it unless there is Dark energy surrounding our visitor."

I closed my eyes and murmured a seeking spell under my breath. It took a second for my magic to connect with the person on my porch. There was something off with the energy, but it wasn't demonic, which was her only concern. She could fight just about every other magical being.

"You're safe. I think they're looking for help finding something."

My mom lifted her hand. "Or fixing something. Remember the last woman needed you to reverse a spell of hers that went awry."

I preferred those that had lost something. Fixing someone else's mistake wasn't easy. Selene was halfway up the stairs by the time I responded to my mother. "Or that. I don't have time right now to help anyone."

Footsteps pounded down the steps. It was too fast. There was no way Selene had gotten to the front door and back in that amount of time. Jean-Marc and the ghoul came into view a second later.

"Hey, mom. There's a guy at the door wanting help with a curse," my son told me.

I had been happy to help magical people when they came to me with an issue, but now was not the time to get involved with someone else's problems. I had a gift to make for the God of the Underworld. Unless it was life-threatening, that trumped everything else at the moment.

"Thanks, buddy. I'll be right there." I turned to Thicket. "Can you draw a design involving a dragon breathing fire that we can put on the shield?" Ever since Nina mentioned a shield, the image refused to leave my mind. I was going with it.

Thicket nodded. "I'd be happy to."

My heart had yet to settle since Aidon dropped the bomb in my lap. My new visitor wasn't helping matters, either. Once I sent the guy home, I would finish the gift and pick out the right clothes to wear when Hades came for dinner.

CHAPTER 3

*J*ean-Marc let the guy in the house and put him in the parlor. It was a safe assumption based on the magical signature coming from the room and the sight of my familiar sitting outside the open french doors.

"Is everything alright?" I directed the silent question to Tarja.

"The man has a nasty curse hanging over his head. I'm surprised he made it past the wards. He means you no harm," she was quick to assure me when I was about to blow up and demand answers to how I could cast more potent wards. *"Otherwise, your protections would have rebuffed him at the driveway."*

I inclined my head and entered the parlor. It was one of the rooms I hadn't made any changes to after moving into the house. Three steps over the threshold, and something slammed into me, knocking me backward. It felt like a sledgehammer to the chest.

I flew through the air and landed hard on my back. The breath was knocked from me, and I laid there praying for my lungs to resume working. Pain radiated out from my shoulder blades and down into my upper back. *Get the fuck up. You were just attacked.*

I gasped, trying to cast a spell. When my voice failed, I kept focusing on my intent and created a bubble of protection around me. I clenched my jaw and rolled over. My lungs relaxed, and I sucked in a breath.

A second later, I spat a spell and pointed at the guy standing with a slack jaw in the doorway to my parlor. "*Vincio!*" The man's blue eyes went wide, and his arms flattened at his side.

Anger raced through my mind, and I prepared to rip into the asshole's mind. His previous genial smile was all bullshit. And that nervousness that wafted off of him like a heavy cologne did its job of disarming me, but the guy would never get the best of me in my own home.

I can't believe I fell for his plea for help. What was wrong with me? I should know better. I thought I'd spelled the property against wolves in sheep's clothing. I paid him back in kind and released a magical blow.

"*Spiro!*" I got grim satisfaction from seeing the guy grunt before flying away from the doorway.

Brushing off my backside, I stalked into the parlor, followed by my familiar. Tarja exuded pride, and it was as I looked down at her that I realized I managed these spells without problems. I was actually getting the hang of this magic stuff! I wanted to shout my accomplishments to the world. This was major for me.

A sense of confidence filled me, and I focused on Tarja. *"Can you go down and protect my family? I've got this guy under control but don't want to leave them vulnerable."*

Her slit green eyes met my gaze, and her tail twitched. It was the only indication she didn't want to leave my side. I'd gotten to know her tells. *"Call me if you need me, and I'll return."*

"I will," I promised, then shifted my focus to the man dressed in khakis and a button-down shirt.

He reminded me of the tech guy at the hospital. Randy was my man whenever I had problems with a terminal or my phone. That calmed some of my anger, and I smiled at him while I remained just inside the entrance to the room.

"What the hell did you do to me? My son said you came for my help, and you attacked me?" I used my harshest 'mom' voice, hoping to frighten the guy.

When he rolled and struggled to climb to his feet, I felt terrible. That didn't mean I fell for his ploy again by rushing to help him. After several awkward seconds, the guy got to his feet and faced me.

"I'm so sorry. I didn't do anything to you. It's the curse. I have no idea what it is or when it will cause problems for me. I'm Stanley Adams, by the way. I've been told you are Phoebe. The new Pleiades witch in town. Someone we can go to for assistance. At least according to my sister-in-law. You helped her best friend Erin with a shifter problem a couple weeks ago."

I lifted one eyebrow. "I wouldn't say I helped Erin all that much. All I really did was help her understand why Alex was stalking her." Shifters had no sense of boundaries when they met the person that they believed was fated for them. That was the case with Alex after running into Erin in a bar. This guy might be legit.

"Tell me how the curse lashed out against me. It makes no sense. From what I know about curses, they're directed to cause the victim problems. Not those around them."

Stan's thin frame shook even more, and his eyes started watering. Whether from frustration, fear, or something else, I couldn't determine. "I have no idea. The witch that cursed me did so because I rejected her. I'm happily married and told her as much. She got pissed and told me no woman would ever get near me again."

God, the poor guy. He was a loyal husband and was punished for it while guys like my ex were out there sleeping with anything younger and in a skirt before kicking me to the curb.

I released the binding spell and extended my hand. The antique coffee table was a broken mess between us, so I had to step over the debris to reach him. Stan shook my hand, giving me a jolt.

I snatched my hand back and rubbed it on my leg before taking a step and putting a bit more space between us. My palm tingled and burned from the contact. That was one helluva curse he was carting around.

"Do you know what she said or did? I'm new to magic and can't break the curse if I don't know what was done to you."

Stan took a deep breath and closed his eyes. His forehead pinched together, and he opened his eyes a second later. "I, uh, I don't know exactly. Something that would make others not want to be around me. Whatever that would be." He seemed lost and confused. Perhaps the enchantment was worse than he realized.

I watched the tall man closely. Stanley had shaggy brown hair and blue eyes and looked like the guy next door. I felt for him and not just because he reminded me of Randy. "The thing is, I will need to do some research on how to break curses. I've never done anything like this and wouldn't want to attempt it without thoroughly looking into the matter. But I cannot do that until after Yule." Having Hades to the house trumped a curse that kept his wife from touching him. Sorry, but it didn't seem like he was in danger of dying anytime soon.

"You can't do that. You have to help me. My wife can't be in the same room as me. She's miserable, and I can't stand seeing her like that. It breaks my heart to see her in pain." There was a frantic edge to Stan's voice, but he wasn't begging me. Odd for a guy that said he was desperate for my help.

"I'm sorry. I wish I had time to help you. Yule is in a few days, and after my visitor leaves, I will be able to do the research and help you. If you need help sooner, I suggest seeking one of the members of the council. I'd bet Lilith could remove the curse."

He dropped his head and clenched his fists at his sides. Energy tickled my senses, putting me on edge. No doubt the curse was reacting to his anger at me over the situation.

"You're the only one that can help me. This isn't something Lilith can do." His insistence told me he might have already gone to the witch with this problem. I'd have to ask her when I talked to her again.

"What did she say? Perhaps she can give you another name because there is no way I can help you right now. I'm just too busy."

Energy pushed against me, and I held my ground. There was a sting to it that told me the curse might lash out again soon. I sucked in a breath and spread my feet apart to keep from being knocked down.

Stanley suddenly hunched over and let out an agonized groan. The veins along his arms bulged like a road map under his skin. I was at his side in an instant and bending over to see how I could help.

I was so focused on Stan's pain that I missed the explosion of energy that signaled a spell. There was no time to process what was happening as an invisible force slammed into the side of my head.

Pain exploded from the point of impact, and my vision

went dark. I couldn't see anything when I flew through the air, the blow having knocked me off my feet. All I could hear was a rapid pounding inside my skull. Dammit. That was twice in one night.

I hit something hard and pointed before I fell to the ground. The leg of the broken table cushioned my body, adding to the agony. I tried to lift my hands to rub my eyes, but they refused to follow my command. They were twitching at my side like popcorn popping in an air fryer with my legs and torso joining in the fun.

"Tarja! I need your help!" I screamed the plea in my mind, but she didn't respond. My gut fell. I tried to pluck our connection. She had to be aware that I'd been hurt.

A foot connected with my side, and I hissed in response, blinking rapidly. Thankfully, the darkness receded, and I was able to see the blurry image of Stanley looming over me like a bad omen.

"Stan...help." My words were whispered and scratchy, like something was stuck in my throat and compressing my vocal cords.

"I wish I could, but I can't." His words shocked me. My legs and arms were still jumping, and my vision cleared a bit more. A second later, I could see his eyes and the grimace on his face. He didn't want to do whatever he was doing. *That's how he got past your wards. He doesn't want to hurt you. Mother trucker. That was a loophole I needed to clear up right away.*

"What?" My chest seized, and I started coughing. "Did you do?" I finally managed to finish.

"What I had to do to save my wife." A look of sorrow crossed his features before he muttered something under his breath. Before I could blink, he dropped a silver charm on my chest and walked out. Heat built between me and the amulet.

I tried to move, but now my entire body had gone stock

still. No more popcorn limbs. I could barely take a full breath. There was a heavy weight on my chest. An astringent odor assaulted my senses right before the charm burned through my sweater. Dammit, I loved this sweater. Jean-Marc gave it to me for my last birthday.

I tried to call out to Tarja again. When she didn't reply, and I could not feel her presence in my mind, I really started to panic. Nothing should come between me and my familiar. Could this charm be the work of Zaleria, the Tainted witch wreaking havoc in my city?

My head hurt, and my vision blurred even worse when I turned my head to look out the doors. I had to make sure Stan was gone. I could tell he had no desire to harm me, but if it meant his wife's life, he would come back in and do even worse to me.

The indistinct form of a cat streaked toward me. "Tarja!" She was here and going to help me. Relief made me dizzy. Or was that the lack of oxygen?

I waited to hear her voice in my mind, but nothing came. When she landed softly on my chest, some of the constriction eased, and my breathing wasn't as shallow as my ex's new girlfriend.

When Tarja batted the charm off my chest, my vision returned along with my ability to move. I sat up, knocking her off my chest in the process. My head swam, so I didn't go far.

Tarja sat by my side and placed a paw on my thigh. Her eyes held concern, and her tail was going faster than the bullet train I took from Dallas to Houston once. Now that I could move my arms, I rubbed the side of my head where I was struck by Stan's spell. My fingers came away wet and sticky.

It took a second for me to process the fact that I was

bleeding. It wasn't dripping down the side of my head, so the injury couldn't be that bad. "What was that?"

Nina came running into the room with wide eyes. "Mom! What happened? Are you alright? Tarja called out to us and said you were attacked."

I gave them a rundown of what happened after Tarja went downstairs. My mother, Nana, Jean-Marc, and Selene had joined me with Mythia and Thicket by the time I was done. "Whatever that charm is, it immobilized me completely."

Mythia flew to my side and recoiled when she got close to the silver circle lying a foot away from me. "That's got some itchy magic."

Nina cocked her head and looked from me to Tarja. "Can you hear what Tarja is saying, mom?"

My familiar's comforting voice was absent from my mind. I couldn't even feel our bond like I usually did. Emotion choked me, making it difficult to speak. "No. I can't hear her at all."

Nina winced and grabbed my hand, giving it a squeeze. "She said no one should touch the charm because it's cursed. And that curse has sunk into you, mom. She feels it invading your entire body."

I jumped to my feet, ignoring the dizziness and pain. None of it mattered as much as getting rid of the curse. I slapped my arms and chest. Jean-Marc was at my side with his hands moving up and down my torso without actually touching me. "How do I get rid of it? I want it gone. Now."

Nina stood up and placed a hand on my shoulder. "There is nothing you can do right now, mom."

"Bullshit. I'm the Pleiades witch. There isn't anything I can't crack," I announced. Jean-Marc wrapped an arm around my shoulders, offering support and comfort.

The front door burst open, and I shoved Nina behind me,

then called my witch fire to my hands. I would incinerate Stanley if he was back for more. I almost dropped the ball of purple flames as my magic went wonky before the fire vanished.

Thankfully, I didn't burn Jean-Marc, who had remained close to my side. The tension in me drained when I saw it was only Layla, a wolf shifter and one of my closest friends, that came running into the entryway.

Fur rippled over Layla's arms while she took in the scene. "I couldn't track him. He was long gone before you reached me, Tarja. I'm sorry." The fur disappeared, and her shoulders lowered.

I gave Layla a condensed version of what happened and told the group Stanley's name. "Does that sound familiar to anyone?"

Layla pursed her lips and tilted her head. "The name isn't familiar to me at all. Hattie has never had any interaction with him.

"Tarja didn't recognize him, either. She said to ask Lilith. She knows every paranormal in town," Nina added.

"We need to locate the son of a bitch so I can get the identity of the Tainted that forced him into cursing me." I wanted to shake him and then kick his ass. He should have told me what was going on. I could have helped his wife.

Nina gasped and shot wide eyes to me. "Even though he didn't want to curse you?"

"He could have told me what was going on and asked for help instead."

My mom lifted a hand. "Not necessarily, Phoebe. I'd bet he was under compulsion to act and something that prevented him from telling you what he was being forced to do."

My gut clenched as I recalled his reactions. He could have been trying to tell me what was going on. "You might be right. I'll figure out what to do with him later. Right now, I need Tarja to give Nina step-by-step instructions on how to break this curse."

Nina's gaze shifted to my familiar. "Tarja says the only way to break it is to find the one who made the object or discover the spell used. We can't undo a curse without knowing what it is," Nina informed us.

This couldn't be happening right before Aidoneus's father was coming to meet me. He would see a pathetic witch incapable of breaking a simple curse on herself and demand his son leave Camden immediately. He might even shatter the enchantment that established the Hellmouth. It was the one way he could sever some of the connection between Aidon and me.

Focus on one catastrophe at a time. Curse first. Hades second. I had no other choice. I didn't want this affecting me when he showed up.

Now that the amulet wasn't in contact with me, I felt fine. Something I know was deceptive because my connection to my familiar was severed. It didn't get much worse than that.

The gods only know what else the spell is doing to me. Could it siphon my magic entirely? I might not have gone into this with my eyes wide open, but I was the Pleaides now, and I loved it. No one was taking that from me.

CHAPTER 4

"Then I guess we'd better hunt him down. He can't have gone far." I was walking to the door before I got the last of my declaration out, anger filling my bloodstream and fueling me. I was going to find this guy and get the answers I needed out of him.

Layla caught up with me on the stairs tossing keys in the air and catching them. "I'll drive. My car is already in the driveway. And Tsekani is still gone in your car, in case you forgot."

I turned my head and gave my friend a smirk. "Honestly, I hadn't thought past finding that asshole. Good thing I'm surrounded by people that have my back."

Layla snorted. "You have like four cars. You'd have taken one of the others."

It was true. I'd inherited four vehicles from Hattie, but I only ever drove the SUV. It was the closest to the Land Rover that was destroyed by Myrna's minions. "I don't drive cars I can barely squeeze into, so I'd have come back and dragged you with me."

Layla laughed as she jumped into the driver's seat of her

red sports car. The wolf in her loved to drive fast and hug the curves. "Fire up those magical senses. It'll help if you can track his signature."

"I'll try. It might help if you drive slower this time."

Layla laughed at me as she peeled out and drove down the driveway. "Nice try, Pheebs. Your intent is what matters. All you need to do is focus on following Stanley with your magic."

"It was worth a try," I grumbled as I grabbed the oh-shit handle and trained my thoughts on following Stan rather than how fast Layla took the curve in the middle of the road leading to my house.

My energy built in my chest before it sputtered and sparked then dissipated. What the heck? I'd gotten so much better at casting lately and hadn't had this problem for months. I must be rattled.

Closing my eyes made my gut churn with nausea. It was better to watch the road while Layla drove. Seeing assured me, we weren't careening off a cliff. That wasn't possible at the moment, so I did my best to shut out the sensations and think about my power and following Stanley.

My energy swirled and was followed swiftly by heat. My blood and body temperature often increased with my magic, but this time it was too rapid. And was soaring far too high. Sweat beaded on my forehead and trickled down my spine. I opened my eyes, expecting my hands to be on fire, but they weren't.

Loud buzzing sounded in my ears, and sharp pain pierced my grey matter. Clutching my head, I looked at Layla for answers. Her lips were moving, but all I heard was a hive of bees in my skull.

I cried out and pressed my palms into my temples. The pain and discomfort made it difficult to remain focused on Stanley and casting a spell to follow him, so I let it go for the moment. As soon as I stopped trying to use my magic, the buzzing dissipated along with the throbbing.

"Phoebe! Are you alright? Can you hear me? Dammit, answer me." Layla slowed the car and pulled over to the side of the road.

I held up a hand and shook my head. "I'm...I don't know." Deep, slow breaths helped eliminate the last of the buzzing. The ache was slower to diminish, but I was able to lift my head and meet her gaze.

"When I tried to access my magic, I was overcome with pain and this awful noise. It was like my head was in a beehive, and I was being stung by long daggers that pierced my parietal, occipital, and frontal bones all at once."

Layla blew out a breath and rolled down the windows. "It has to be the curse. There's no other reason you would be experiencing these symptoms. Tarja is saying the curse is worse than we thought."

My stomach dropped to my feet. Turning away, I looked out the window. We were parked on the main road leading to my house. There were no signs of anything out of the ordinary on either side of us.

Ever since I'd inherited the Pleaides magic, I could sense what was around me. At first, I had no idea what it was. Tarja had explained what all the input meant. However, I didn't truly get it until Aidon, and I were roaming around Mount Battie looking for Lilith.

While in the wilderness, I had to tap into those senses and scan what creatures surrounded us, looking not only for Lilith but also for enemies. It had come in handy, and I had been using it ever since. Most of the time, it was automatic.

The buzzing and pain started up again when I tried to get a sense of the magic surrounding us. It wasn't bad, but it was uncomfortable. Most of all, I was struck by the absence of any input. It took me back to my days as a powerless mundie.

"I've got nothing. I can't even detect the magical signature of creatures that might be close to us. It's as if Hattie never gave me anything." My heart was racing at the same time my chest constricted. I couldn't catch my breath, and my mind raced to find a way back to my power. I didn't want to lose it. It was part of me now, and I liked who I had become.

Layla put her hand on my thigh. "Except Hattie did give you her power. You haven't lost it. The pain and noise are proof enough of that. Tarja assures me this is all the curse. She said to tell you we will not stop until we have you back to normal."

I'd been a mundie all my life. It had never stopped me before, so I wouldn't let this setback hinder my progress now. I took a deep breath and rubbed my face. "Alright. What do we do now? Can you try and track him by scent? I have no desire to drive around endlessly for hours, but I will if you think you got enough from the house."

"I definitely got a nose full in the house, but unless he has his windows down, I doubt we will get much." Layla got out of the vehicle and stood on the side of the road with her hands on her hips.

I climbed out and leaned on the roof of the car, watching her from the passenger side. It fascinated me when her eyes shifted shape and darkened while her nostrils flared. She sniffed the air, turning this way and that.

After a few seconds, she turned around and shook her head. The look on her face was a hammer through the thin pane of hope that sparked in my chest. It was difficult not to get caught up in defeat and simply give up.

"It was a long shot. Maine in the winter isn't windows-down weather." It was downright freezing this time of year. "Let's figure out the next steps in the car with the heater on. My fingers are going numb."

Layla inclined her head and ducked into the driver's seat.

By the time I sat down, she had the windows up and the heater blasting. I held my popsicle digits in front of the vents and considered how we might be able to find Stanley.

"What about driving around the neighborhoods that have a higher paranormal population?" Layla beat me to the punch with that suggestion. "Jean-Marc said he drove a black Ford pick-up truck. I can pick up his scent if we find the right vehicle. We just need a starting point, and that seems like the best to me."

"Jean-Marc saw what he was driving? And he told us?" I hadn't heard that before we got in her car and left.

"Yeah, he let the guy into the house. A fact that is filling him with guilt, Tarja says. Anyway, he just told them what he saw, and Tarja told me."

That was a relief. Losing my connection to my magic was bad enough. If I was losing my mind as well, that would be catastrophic. My best bet at finding the solution to this mess was my quick, strategic mind.

"Now that we know what we're looking for, your plan makes even more sense. At least now we know what we are searching for, so we aren't going in totally blind." I wanted to tell her the plan was like trying to find a needle in a haystack but didn't. It was the only way forward we had at the moment. And I needed to do something. I couldn't sit there waiting until this curse robbed me of my magic.

Layla pulled onto the highway and headed into town. I got lost in dark thoughts that refused to let me go. By the time she turned down the street where Stella and I encountered the witch sisters haunting their family home, I was convinced the gift Hattie gave me would be ripped from me, killing my children in the process then me.

Layla's hand covered mine, where it gripped my thigh. "It's going to be alright. Freaking out won't help you right now. Curses can do a lot of things, but they can be beaten. And we will overcome this one, too."

"But what if we don't find the answer before it kills me...and my kids?"

Layla shot me a furrowed brow before she refocused on the road. "Your kids weren't cursed, Pheebs. They are fine. And this is not going to kill you. We won't let it."

I willed my heart to slow and the vice around my chest to loosen. It amazed me how quickly I'd forgotten my vow to beat this problem. In my defense, thoughts of something harming my kids gave me tunnel vision.

"That's right. This bitch isn't going to win this round either. You know, she messed up by constantly attacking me. It's made me act on my feet and taken her best weapon away. Fear often cripples you. After everything, I've learned to keep fighting despite the terror I might feel."

Layla chuckled as she slowed to a crawl. "Your ability to keep going is one of the things I admire about you. It took me decades to be as capable as you."

I fluff my hair as I scan the vehicles parked in the driveways. "That's one perk of being middle-aged. You learn you have to adapt or get run over by life. And you get good at it, as well. I just wish it didn't come with fine lines and the need for Spanx. These things are like boa constrictors around my thighs and waist."

We drove throughout the neighborhood without any luck. When we reached Lilith's house, I asked Layla to pull over. "Let's go ask Lilith if she knows Stanley Adams."

"If anyone knows, she will. That witch is a busy body." Layla climbed out of the car and slammed her door.

I followed suit and walked up the path to the front door. I lifted my hand to knock but the door opened before my fist made contact. Lilith was standing there in a navy business suit with a scowl on her face. "To what do I owe the pleasure? We didn't have a meeting scheduled until Friday."

"You're right, but I've got a problem that I'm hoping you can help me with. Can we come inside?" I glanced to the left, then the right, making sure no one was near to hear me say that. I didn't think the Pleaides should be asking for help so openly.

Lilith stepped aside and held the door open. "Would you like something to drink?"

I walked past her, followed by Layla. "No, thank you. We won't take much of your time. I need to ask if you know someone."

Lilith closed the door and entered a living room to the right of the entrance. "Who is that?"

I took a seat on the couch and waited for her to take the loveseat across from me. "Stanley Adams came to visit me tonight and asked for help with a curse. I fell for his charade and would like to pay him a visit."

Lilith's piercing hazel eyes saw right through me. "What did this Stanley Adams do? Your magic is off."

I released a sigh then gave her a brief rundown of the events leading up to this moment. "I cannot break this curse until I find Stanley and make him tell me who forced him to act against me, so do you know him?"

Lilith's features tightened to the point I worried her skin was going to split open. "There is no Stanley Adams in the magical world. I suspect he used a fake name. What did he look like?"

I should have known it wasn't going to be this easy. I didn't freaking have time for this. Hades was due to visit soon. "He was slim, about six feet tall. And had shaggy brown hair and blue eyes. Honestly, he reminded me of a tech nerd."

Lilith pursed her lips and tapped her knee for a few seconds. "He doesn't sound familiar, but I will ask around. If something happened to his wife, someone might have noticed her absence. There is a chance he isn't from Camden, so I will ask contacts outside the area, as well."

Given that my magical contacts lived across the pond, I appreciated her effort. "Thanks, Lilith. Please give me a call if you hear anything."

We took our leave and were walking back to the car when movement caught my eye. An imp with one broken horn was bouncing in the shrubs next to Lilith's house. "Layla. Over there!"

Layla growled and followed my finger. The imp jumped from the ground into the tree in the middle of the yard. "I've got it!"

Lilith came running out of her front door at the moment Layla shifted, shredding her clothing. And I stood there with my thumb up my ass. I couldn't do anything to help. "Can you hide her? Not everyone around is paranormal."

Sadness crossed Lilith's features before she nodded and lifted her hands. *"Subripio!"* Energy rippled from Lilith's outstretched hands and shimmered in the air at the border of her lawn. I saw the spell take hold and felt the magic of it once it was in place.

Even though it hadn't been very long, I missed my abilities more than I ever could have imagined. A thought that only made me more determined. "Holy shit!" Layla jumped onto the lowest branch and started clawing at the limbs above her head. Leaves and sticks rained down.

"Dammit," Lilith cursed. A neighbor's door opened, and someone gasped, drawing our attention. *"Indistinctus!"* The guy's mouth closed, and he glanced around, then waved to Lilith and went back inside his house.

"Mundie?" I asked while I watched the imp bounce around the tree in the yard. Where the hell had it come from?

Demonic activity had been minimal since Aidoneus, and I installed the Hellmouth.

"Yes. Darren is mundane and in everyone's business. He won't trust what he saw, given that we look like we're standing here calmly having a conversation. Why is there an imp in my yard? Did it follow you?"

I jerked my head back, and my eyebrows scrunched as I considered her question. "I'm not sure. I want to say I doubt it, but I lost my ability to sense anything around me, in addition to my magic. Layla would have noticed, but she's been too worried about me."

Lilith put her hand on my shoulder and squeezed. "I'm sorry this is happening to you. I'm not sure why anyone would want to curse you. They can't steal your power for themselves that way. As you know, a Pleaides must give her power away freely."

I shrugged my shoulders. "Perhaps they want me neutralized for their next steps. If I can't access my power, I can't stop them."

Lilith's pale face lost all color. "That would be incredibly bad. We have to find Stanley Adams and get the information right away. Yule would be the perfect night to make a move. Everyone will be side-tracked by their celebrations. And the coven will be gathered in one place."

Layla landed in front of us, making Lilith screech. She cast another spell right before her neighbor peeked through his front curtains. I threw my head back and laughed to cover her fright.

Sobering, I grimace when I see the bloody body hanging from Layla's jaws. "Good job, Layla. I'll get you some clothes and a bag for that." A shudder moved through me as I pointed to the dead demon.

"I don't have anything that will fit her," Lilith sniffed.

I snorted and shook my head. "Layla would rather drive

naked than wear your clothes. But I would like a plastic garbage bag if you have one."

"I wouldn't wear her clothing, either," Lilith pointed out. "I'll be right back."

Glancing down at Layla, I pointed to the ground. "Drop that right there and don't move. I'm going to grab your extra clothes."

I took off down the walkway and popped the trunk. As a shifter, Layla carries a few extra sets of clothes in her car for emergency purposes. I grab the stuff on top and swipe the white gym towel, as well.

Lilith was back with a pair of tongs and a white bag. I toss Layla the clothes and take the implements from Lilith. "Thanks." The demon's black blood was already killing the lawn where Layla dropped it. I had no desire to ruin Lilith's tongs, so I handed them back and put my hand in the bag, then used it like a glove to pick up the imp-like he was a pile of poop.

Keeping my hold on the limp body, I yanked my hand and turned the bag around it. I wrapped the plastic around the demon several times and tied the top off. I wasn't sure if it was actually dead. These suckers were hard to kill, so I would take it to Aidoneus to deal with.

I'd hit my limit for the day and needed a long, hot bath. What I really wish I could do is hit the rewind button and go back to obsessively cleaning before Stanley showed up and cursed me.

CHAPTER 5

I forced my feet up the porch stairs and into my house. The day had exhausted me. It started at o-dark-thirty this morning when I started my cleaning spree. It had only gone downhill from there.

My mom walked out of the kitchen with a towel in her hands. "How did it go? Did you find Stanley?"

I shook my head and passed her as I entered the kitchen in search of my cell phone. I left so hastily earlier that I had forgotten to bring it with me. "We found an imp prowling around Lilith's house, but we never located Mr. Adams. I might strangle the man when I get my hands on him."

My mom turned away from me and focused on the corner. When I bent and looked around her, I saw Tarja sitting in the living room with Nana. I was about to ask what was going on when my mom swiveled to face me once again. "Tarja wants to know if the imp was following you guys or hunting Lilith."

"I can't answer that because I wasn't able to track it using my magical senses. Those seem to be gone, as well. Although I doubt it is a coincidence, it was there when I was. Lilith shouldn't be a target of anyone since there's a good chance she hates me." I dropped the bag onto the counter and turned to the fridge for my bottle of water.

"No!" I shouted when I saw Mythia going for the bag from the corner of my eye.

The tiny pixie squeaked and darted away from the white plastic. "What did I do?"

"Sorry, Thia. That's the dead imp. I didn't want you to open it and drop it on the kitchen counter. I don't think we could ever get it clean after that toxic blood hit it." I shuddered from the mere thought of such a thing.

Jean-Marc walked through the door leading down to my workroom. "What's going on? I heard you shouting, mom."

Mythia pointed at the bag on the counter. "She was stopping me from seeing a dead imp."

"I still have the taste of that thing in my mouth," Layla complained as she walked to the fridge and grabbed a coke.

Jean-Marc lifted one brow and moved closer to the island. "Imp as in demon? I thought you and your boyfriend created the Hellmouth to keep demons in the Underworld and away from Earth."

"We did," I told him. "This little guy could have been here before. Or not. It's not like the seal is foolproof. The lower demons had an easier time crossing before. Maybe it's the same now."

My mom came over and placed her hand on my shoulder. "Are you feeling okay? You know it's next to impossible for demons to cross here. But they can cross further away from the Hellmouth and make their way here if their summoner orders them to."

I stared at my mother for a few seconds. "Of course. It's been a long day. That's all. I need to call Aidoneus and have him take care of this carcass."

I grabbed my cell from the charger on the small built-in

desk off to the side of the kitchen. I pulled up his contact and hit send before anyone could corner me and ask more questions.

A smile spread across my face when I heard Aidon's sultry voice through the phone. "Hello, Queenie. Miss me already?"

I chuckled at his question. "If it hadn't been so busy here today, I'd probably miss you a lot right now." We hadn't spent much time together for the past week since Jean-Marc came home from college for a visit.

I heard him gasp through the speaker and imagined his hand flew to his chest. He could be dramatic sometimes. I supposed that was part of being a god. "The luster is wearing off already?"

"I wouldn't say that. Between having a mini-meltdown over your father's pending visit, going on a cleaning spree, being attacked and cursed, I haven't had time to think about a whole lot."

"You were cursed? When? Where?" All teasing had vanished from the tone of his voice. He was one hundred percent alpha male at the moment.

"I can fill you in later. We are dealing with that issue. What I need from you is your help dealing with a dead imp. Layla killed it while we were visiting Lilith a bit ago."

Layla leaned over my shoulder and put her mouth close to the phone. "Speaking of demons. Have any crossed through the Hellmouth lately? We aren't sure if it was following us from the house or already close to Lilith's."

Aidoneus growled, the sound promising a violent death. "The Hellmouth has been silent since we created it. They aren't being summoned in this town. But that doesn't mean witches and demons aren't finding a location where the barrier is weakened. I'll be over soon, love. Then I want to hear all about this curse."

"Thank you." I hung up before he could say anything else to me. By the time I faced the kitchen again, my entire family was present and looking at me. "He's coming over. And he said demons aren't crossing in Camden."

The doorbell rang, saving me from another interrogation. I didn't have the strength to deal with it anymore right now. Singing echoed from behind the closed panel, making me smile. Christmas carolers were rare nowadays. Some church groups would go around to member homes and sing, but on the whole, it was a tradition that was dying in popularity.

Yanking the door open, I smiled when I saw the group of men and women standing there holding folders in their hands. They were belting out Santa's Coming to Town while a few rang bells.

My eyes traveled to the woman in the middle of the group. She wore a brown jacket with a green and blue scarf around her neck and a green beanie on her head. I immediately started humming along with them.

A verse into the song, time seemed to stop as the world receded from around me. My stomach fluttered before joy took me over. I loved the holidays. It brought families and friends together and gave you a chance to shower them with love.

Have I done my shopping yet? Did I even need to buy anything? I couldn't recall if there was anyone to buy presents for or not. Their song shifted, and my body swayed from side to side. It was beautiful.

Something tugged on my arm, making me yank it away. I wanted to stand right here listening to the music. A young woman with long brown hair and brown eyes stepped between the carolers and me. She wasn't singing.

Instead, she put her hands on my shoulders and pushed me. I stumbled and gaped at her as she closed the door on the people outside. "Why did you do that?"

She put her hands on her hips and leaned her head toward me. "Because you were letting the cold air in the house. What's wrong with you?"

"I was listening to the carolers sing songs. Have you lost all your holiday spirit? Wait. Why are you at my house? Who are you?" I snarled at her and waved my hands. There was a table behind her with a large glass vase filled with beautiful flowers. As I was waving my hands, the glass exploded, and water and flowers went everywhere.

The girl's eyes flew wide, and in a flash, I was surrounded by four or five people. One was an older lady and her daughter. Then there was a young man that resembled the one that pushed me. There was also a wolf and a tiny little fairy flying next to the young man.

I screamed and tried to run away. "Don't hurt me. I'll give you anything you want."

The young man grabbed my shoulders and stopped me. "Mom, stop it. You're safe. You know us. I'm your son, Jean-Marc, and that's your daughter, Nina."

No wonder the young woman talked to me like that. I didn't remember them. My heart started racing with that knowledge. "And that's your mother and your grandmother," Jean-Marc finished.

"Did someone drug my drink?" It was the only thing that made sense. "I can't remember anything. And, I seem to be seeing things."

Jean-Marc shook his head. "No one drugged your drink. What are you seeing?"

"Do you remember who you are?" The woman he said was my mother asked.

A tiny man was hammering against the inside of my skull, making my headache. I grabbed it and almost fell down as I swayed back and forth. Jean-Marc steadied me. "No! I don't even know my name! Something is seriously wro...ahhh!

That wolf just turned into a naked woman. Oh God, what is happening to me?"

Jean-Marc shifted his gaze to the others surrounding us. His expression screamed that he was panicking. My grandmother grabbed my hand and tugged me further into the house. "Let's have a seat in the living room, and we can talk about everything. Right now, you don't look so good, sweetheart." My racing heart warmed at her term of endearment. But I didn't know this lady, so I pulled my hand away and tried to back away from them. I could run out the front door.

When I bumped into someone, I glanced back and saw Jean-Marc. Not wanting to upset these people if they really were my kids, I followed the old lady into a room filled with couches and a TV. I sat on the end of the sofa closest to the exit while everyone else filed into the room, followed by a large tabby cat. I didn't own a cat. Where did it come from?

Nina's voice distracted me. "Long story short. You're a powerful witch, mom, and someone cursed you."

My jaw dropped to my chest. "What the hell are you talking about?" I wanted to shout a denial, but something stopped me. Maybe she was right. Something was wrong with me, and it wasn't drugs. I'd have more impairments if it was.

"We don't have time to tell you everything, Phoebe. I'll give you a condensed version," my grandmother interjected. "The woman you were caring for, Hattie Silva, gave you her magic to save your life, and you became a powerful witch. Others are jealous of your power and want to take it from you. Someone cursed you today, and it cut you off from your power."

A knock echoed from the back of the house. A masculine voice called out after I heard a door open and close. "Phoebe. You here? Where is everyone?"

"In here," my grandmother called out.

"Are you sure he should see her like this, Nana?" My son asked.

"He's a god. He's our best bet of getting her help right now."

The sexiest guy I'd ever seen walked into the room, stealing my breath. I couldn't look away from his tousled black hair and stunning sapphire eyes. "What shouldn't I see? Hello, Queenie. You don't look so hot." He was looking directly at me, so I assumed he was talking to me. Knowing he found me unattractive made me wince and lower my head.

"She isn't herself, Aidoneus." That was my grandmother's voice. "She answered the door earlier to some carolers and went blank. She has no idea who we are or who she is at the moment. Tarja didn't think it was the mundies at the door, but the curse taking full effect. She postulated that it took longer because it had to work past Phoebe's natural defenses."

"Fuck," Aidoneus cursed. "She sounded off when we spoke, which is why I came right over. I should be back at the Hellmouth to welcome my father, but I knew something was wrong. What do you guys know?"

I peered through the fall of my hair and lowered my gaze again when I saw Aidoneus looking right at me. A finger pressed in the underside of my chin, forcing my face to lift. "Look at me, gorgeous. You remember me?"

I looked into his eyes and swore he could see all the way to my soul. I felt naked around him, but it didn't scare me. It felt natural. Which made no sense because I couldn't remember ever meeting him.

"You feel familiar, but I have no memories of you," I admitted.

Aidoneus went to his knees in front of me and grabbed my hands. He closed his eyes, and my hands started tingling.

It felt like his fingers were moving across every inch of my body, and I loved it. I never wanted him to stop.

Unfortunately, he opened his eyes, and the sensations all stopped. He shifted his gaze to the cat, of all things. "This is no ordinary curse. It was created with Blood magic. I'm not familiar enough with it to suggest a solution. Do you know who cast the curse?"

My grandmother shook her head from side to side. "We have a name that might be fake. All we know for sure is that the guy came here looking for help with a curse he claimed was placed on him. He attacked Phoebe and dropped a cursed charm on her chest that burnt through her clothes and skin. He told her he did it to save his wife, so he was under duress."

Wow. All of that happened to me. It sure sounded like it would explain why I was feeling lost and confused right now. I wanted to doubt these people, but they sounded legitimate. There was no hesitation in her explanation, and she held his gaze throughout.

Aidoneus lifted my hands to his mouth and pressed a kiss to the back of them. "How did he get past her wards? Imps can't even get past them. Speaking of. Where's the dead imp. I want to make sure it isn't part of the problem."

The fairy flew away then returned a second later, carrying a white bag that was ten times bigger than her. I'd never seen anyone so tiny manage that much weight. She dropped the bag into Aidoneus's hands.

"Thank you, Mythia," Aidoneus replied as he opened the plastic.

I glanced down with him and jumped onto the back of the couch when I saw a miniature devil with its head hanging on by mere threads. The sight was revolting, and it smelled like a sewer.

Aidoneus set the bag down and knelt on the cushion in

front of me. "It's alright, love. It looks like Layla killed the imp. It won't hurt you."

A knock at the door made me jump again. My grandmother cursed and pushed up from her recliner. "I'm tired of the doorbell ringing today. Every time has been one more disaster. Don't you magical people know it's the holidays? We should have peace and quiet."

My mother motioned for my grandmother to sit back down. "I've got it, mother." Jean-Marc followed my mom out of the room.

Aidoneus stood up and went to the entrance to the living room, and looked out. He was walking away a second later. "Father. What are you doing here? I left word that I would return as soon as possible."

"You think I was going to ignore the fact that my son was dealing with some kind of emergency with this mundane woman turned witch? It's bad enough she stole you from us. The last thing I will tolerate is her causing you harm." Aidoneus's father's voice resonated through me like I was sitting in front of speakers at a concert.

It rattled my insides and made me shiver. Add to that the fact that he seemed to glow. It seemed as if a spotlight was shining behind him. My eyes burned when I looked directly at him. The guy was packing some serious power. I might not know much, but that was undeniable.

"Dad, turn off the high beams. You don't need to intimidate these people. They're my friends. Go back to my house. Now. And for the record, Phoebe isn't hurting anyone. She's the one that has been hurt." Aidoneus sounded like he was moving closer to the living room.

Another guy walked into the room wearing a scowl as he glanced around at everyone. The guy had perfectly chiseled features, black hair, and dark eyes. He looked a lot like a sexy movie star that played a werewolf in a popular series. Only the god standing in my house wore a five-piece suit that likely cost more than my house rather than ratty jeans and flannel shirts.

"Which one is she? The naked one or the catatonic one?" His words were harsh, and he lifted one corner of his mouth as if he didn't like what he saw. My memory might be gone, but I knew enough to know his disdain wasn't my problem.

Another fairy flew into the room. This one was a guy, and he was carrying a small silver knife. He looked around the room, let out a squeak and dropped the weapon before he took off. Aidoneus picked up the blade and stuck it into his back pocket.

"Dad, Phoebe has been cursed. She isn't catatonic, but she also isn't herself right now." The naked woman grabbed the blanket from the back of the couch and wrapped it around herself when Aidoneus distracted his dad.

Aidoneus's father sneered at me. "How could a powerful Pleiades witch allow herself to fall into a trap like that? Your abilities should prevent you from falling victim to something so sinister."

"That's enough," Aidoneus bellowed. "You will respect Phoebe. She is new to magic and learning everything she can as fast as she can."

My grandmother crossed her arms over her chest. "I'll have you know that my granddaughter is more advanced than expected after having magic less than a year, Hades." She sneered his name, making me smile. Some of my feelings were coming back. I loved her deeply. Now, if I could remember some details.

"She was trying to help someone that was being coerced into harming her. As the God of the Underworld, I would think you would show more appreciation for such compassion. Isn't that rare in your world?" My Nana just insulted the God Hades.

My heart raced for my grandmother. If this guy was the actual devil, he might kill us all for her disrespect. I jumped in front of her, ready to take the blow if he attacked. Aidoneus moved between his father and us and cupped my face in his palms.

"Don't worry, love. I won't let anything happen to you or your family. But I'm glad to see your reaction. It assures me you're in there somewhere. We just need to find a way to remove the Blood curse."

I glanced over his shoulder at his father and wondered what my life was like that two gods were standing in my living room. I had to be this powerful witch. No way would gods visit an average person.

CHAPTER 6

"*A* Blood curse is no excuse not to be prepared for my visit. This lack of welcome and this hovel is insulting. You're hosting a God. I expect the best, and you deliver filth." Aidoneus's father was a bit of an asshole. Pretentious and demanding. I'd worked hard to prepare for his arrival, and he insulted me by looking down his nose at me.

A gasp escaped me, and I shot a happy grin at my family. "I remember going on a cleaning rampage this morning and agonizing over Hades coming to visit." I turn to face the god now.

"Although, now I can't for the life of me understand why I was so worried. My family deserves the effort, but you surely don't. Not if you can't appreciate that not everyone has unlimited resources. My house is not a hovel. It's a mansion in my world, and I'm damn proud of what my family and I have built. You know where the door is if you're that uncomfortable."

Aidoneus laughed and gathered me into his arms. I wrapped my arms around his neck as he lifted me off the back of the couch where I was still perched. The happiness of a moment ago morphed into desire, and I was all too willing when he pressed his lips to mine.

The ache in my head vanished as he kissed me passionately. I felt his love and affection for me in every stroke of his tongue and caress of his hand. It warmed me and brought me back to who I was.

Memory flooded my mind and brought reason with it. I broke the kiss, now very aware of my children watching us. Aidoneus's blue eyes were liquid heat as he smiled down at me and set me down.

"This woman is not only cursed but delusional," Hades declared behind me.

I released Aidoneus and turned around to face the angry God. Nana approached me along with my mother and both of my kids. Layla entered the room a second later, along with Selene.

"I'm sorry you don't feel at home here. I'd planned on making a feast to welcome you, but some witch had other plans. And this house is far better than the hotel I was living in before moving back to Camden."

Aidon's hands on my shoulders grounded me. "Your house is not the issue here. Queenie. What I want to know is how you gained your memory back? When I arrived, you had no memory of who you were, let alone the rest of us."

I lifted my hands into the air, and I took a few steps away. I needed space to keep a clear head and test a theory. "Honestly, I have no idea. It started when Nana talked to your dad but didn't fully come back until you picked me up."

"Can you use your magic now?" My son asked. Jean-Marc was standing between his sister and Hades and kept casting covert glances at the god.

"Let me try. I'm not getting my hopes up, though. From the sound of it, curses aren't that easy to remove," I tell my son.

It was difficult to ignore the snort of derision from the God in our midst. Hades' power was a burning beacon in our midst. Blinding and suffocating at the same time. It also smelled like the forest after heavy rain. Guess I was wrong about him bathing in brimstone.

There was a scented balsam candle on the coffee table, and I focused on trying to light the three wicks. I conjured an image of the top layer of wax melted until it was translucent while the flames glowed softly. Clearing my mind was far more difficult, but eventually, I managed.

"Incendo." The spell was a whisper from my lips that wasn't accompanied by the usual bubbling rush of energy when I cast.

I shifted my gaze to Tarja. "I can't do it. I can't even feel my magic anymore. Could I have lost it?"

Her feline eyes never left mine, but I never heard her response in my head. I missed her intrusions, lessons, and advice. Most of all, I missed her scratchy laughter. We had plans. We were going to fix the familiar spirit realm so they could procreate again. My magic couldn't be gone.

Nina twined her fingers with mine. "She says your magic is still there because she is still bonded to you. If you no longer had the power, I would now hold the Pleaides position, and her bond would have shifted to me. The fact that it hasn't means there is hope."

"Unless it takes so long to find the solution that the pent-up magic burns through her frontal cortex, leaving her a vegetable." I gaped at Hades' casual declaration.

Aidoneus snarled and pushed his father in the chest. "Why do you have to be an asshole today? Phoebe has done nothing to deserve your hatred. All she has done from the moment her life was turned upside down is sacrifice her happiness for everyone else. She's been attacked several hundred times and nearly died far more often than I care to recall."

"It's true. She gets a discount at the hospital for being a frequent visitor," Nana added.

I let go of Nina's hand and rubbed my temples. "Is that possible? Can the energy scramble my brains like eggs?"

Aidoneus was in front of me and grabbing my shoulders in the blink of an eye. "Yes, it can. All energy needs an outlet."

"So, it's like a balloon. If you fill it too full, it'll pop," Jean-Marc observed. The deep grooves around his mouth and eyes spoke volumes about his anger. "How much time do we have?"

"That's difficult to answer. It's different for everyone," Aidon explains.

"But your mother will have less time than most because she harnesses a significant amount of power. Far more than even demigods have at their disposal. That's why it had to be broken up and shared with so many," his father interrupted. "That power almost destroyed the godly realm."

"You might be the father of the god Phoebe is dating. He's someone we've come to love too. But that doesn't give you the right to be a sanctimonious asshole relishing the idea that my granddaughter will become a vegetable because of some curse. Have some damn empathy."

The veins running down Hades' neck bulged and throbbed when he clenched his jaw. Aidon scowled at his father, who lost his anger and rolled his eyes. "I'm only reporting the truth." The God of the Underworld was trying to placate his son. It humanized him and made me worry for my Nana's safety just a bit less.

"You're right. And I appreciate the information. It's not all that surprising." I'd known the history behind the creation of witches and mages. Hades could have been gentler, but he was trying to get a rise out of me. Too bad for him it was only pissing me off. "Lilith is searching for Stanley, as well. We'll have answers soon."

"I've called Tsekani. I'm going to head back out and do another search for the black truck," Layla interjected. "We won't stop until we find him."

"How do you know he'll give you the information you need?" Nina was chewing on her lower lip, and her shoulders were hunched. I wrapped my arm around her shoulders and kissed the top of her head.

"I've dealt with your father. Over twenty years of marriage followed by a bitter divorce taught me how to handle assholes. Stanley Adams will be putty in my hands." I regretted my words the moment I said them. "Not that I'm saying anything bad about your father."

Jean-Marc's smile didn't reach his eyes. "Yes, you are, mom. And you should. He cheated on you for god knows how long, then had his skanky girlfriend fire you then ban you from area hospitals. Asshole's too nice a term to describe him."

I grab my son's hand. "He's still your father. But he's not the point right now. I'm confident in my ability to force the information from Stanley, even without my magic."

"You won't be facing him alone." Aidoneus's promise didn't come as a surprise, but his father's lack of a response did. I didn't trust Hades when he was silent.

"I will be in contact if I find anything." With that announcement, Layla left the house.

Mythia flew closer to Aidoneus. She hovered in front of him, wringing her hands. "Is this a good time to have you deal with the dead imp? I don't want to start dinner with it in the kitchen."

Hades lifted a brow. "An imp got through the Hellmouth? Perhaps you were wrong to trust the collaboration with the witch. We can return the veil to its previous state easily enough."

"You need to give up on the attempts to break us up. There is nothing I wouldn't do for your son. I'd die protecting him, and I know he would do the same for me. We love each other. Something that's rare no matter what realm you come from, and I won't take it for granted or give it up. Not for anyone or anything." I tried to calm the trembling in my body. The last thing I wanted was for Hades to think I was afraid of him. He didn't need to know I was about to pee my pants because I was scared of him.

I mean, the god could wave a hand and kill every single person in the house. But I couldn't stand by and let him think it was alright to try and come between Aidoneus and me. I might not have known what we were to each other before. That changed the second his father began his campaign to split us up.

Love was a precious gift. Something that should be nurtured and cherished. It was the one thing that mattered at the end of your life. The size of your bank account didn't make one bit of difference in the end. Your house wouldn't stand up for you or take care of you when you were sick. Your loved ones did that for you.

"I feel the same way, dad. You and mom have shown me what true love looks like. It took thousands of years, but I discovered that with Phoebe. It insults me when you try to convince me she isn't the woman for me. I know you understand what I'm saying. I believe my grandmother did the same to you and mom."

Emotion crossed Hades' face when Aidoneus mentioned his mom. Unfortunately, it was gone so quickly I doubted it made an impact on the god. "I can see why you like her, son. There's a fire in her gut. Much like your mother."

It took an effort to keep my jaw from hitting the floor.

That was the last thing I expected to hear from him. Aidoneus chuckled and clapped his dad on the shoulder. "She's just as feisty as mom. Independent, too. It's infuriating at times how she insists on doing everything on her own. But it's also one of the things I fell in love with in the first place."

"Now that you've found common ground," my mom began as she got to her feet and faced Aidoneus. "Is there any way for us to help restore the link between Phoebe and Tarja? I'm concerned about the build-up of energy and think her familiar can help siphon the excess away to keep her from having her frontal cortex fried."

"That's...I hadn't considered that recourse. I'm not entirely certain it will make a difference. The familiar-witch bond is symbiotic, with one assisting the other in a continual loop. It's worth a try." Hades sounded surprised when he spoke. I imagined he was shocked a simple human woman had a suggestion that hadn't crossed his mind.

Tarja had been protecting me from the moment I received the magic. I imagined she could help with this. "How do we open the line again? I think we need to move fast. The headache is returning, and my body hurts all over again."

Nina's focus shifted to Tarja, and her head started bobbing up and down. "Tarja said it would be easiest to have Aidoneus scan the magical chain that links the two of you for obstacles. Unlike your magic in general, your bond to her is contained in one place. His bond with you should give him the ability to find this."

"What do you think?" I held my breath as I waited for Aidon to respond.

"It's the best idea I've heard all night. I was about to go join the search. It's killing me to sit here and do nothing. We should have Nina and Jean-Marc cast a circle and call the elements. Asking for Hecate's blessing will improve chances of success," Aidon replied.

Nina squealed and raced for the kitchen. "I'll grab the salt and herbs. You clear the floor, Jean-Marc." The last of her words were shouted as she raced away.

Nana went over to her recliner in the corner, and my mother perched on the arm of the sofa that wouldn't be in the way. I pushed the coffee table out past Hades, with Selene helping me while Jean-Marc moved the loveseat. When I returned, Aidoneus was rolling up the carpet.

Nina was back and handing a container to Jean-Marc. "You spread this out in a circle with mom, Aidoneus, and Tarja in the middle. And I will call the elements."

To my surprise, Hades sat on the couch near my mom. It seemed odd seeing him sit on an old leather sofa. Accepting his silence as another good sign, I walked to the middle of the open space. Aidon and Tarja joined me while Selene and Mythia watched from the archway leading to the kitchen.

Nina placed white candles at the cardinal points, and Jean-Marc sprinkled the salt and herb mixture around us. White light flashed when he completed his task. Nina lit the candles with magic, then paused and held her hands out at her sides.

"Hear me, Guardians of the East, the element of Air. We call you tonight with an open heart and clear voice to ask that you lend your knowledge. Guardians of the South, the Element of Fire we call to thee. We ask for assistance with lighting the passions within to connect more deeply with the world around us. Guardians of West, Element of Water. We call you today to lend your emotion and purity to this ritual. Guardians of the North, Powers of Earth, we call to thee and ask that you gift us with your steadfastness and manifestation during this ritual. Enter here and welcome." When Nina finished the chant, the wind whipped through the circle, and the flames rose toward the ceiling.

Aidoneus grabbed my hands while Tarja stood between us. He closed his eyes and chanted something in ancient Greek. It sent heat traveling up my arms and into my chest. My skin tingled, and some of the weight in my soul lightened.

The weight was back a second later, followed by pain. I bit my cheek to keep from crying out. I needed to allow Aidoneus to do his thing. It seemed like he stood there for hours. Eventually, I heard faint whispers.

I glanced down at Tarja. *"Can you hear me?"* I cried out in relief and let go of Aidon's hand.

"I heard that. It was faint, but there." A part of me had worried I would never hear her voice again. My mother had given me hope with her suggestion. I believed in those around me, but not being connected to Tarja made it seem impossible.

Aidon wiped the sweat from his brow. "I'm not sure I can remove more of the block along your path. It was like trying to lift a hundred-story building with one finger. I shifted it to the side and cleared a sliver. That's why I think she sounds faint and is also why I'm not certain she will be able to siphon energy to help give us time."

I cupped his cheeks. "Doesn't matter. You've done enough. I have her voice back. We will beat this."

"I can feel the excess Hades talked about. I've tried to pull it toward me but haven't been successful yet. I will keep trying. Even if all I draw is a small amount, it will help your discomfort."

I bent and picked Tarja up, cradling her to my chest. "Thank you, mom. I always knew you were the smartest among us. Who's hungry? I know I'm starved."

Mythia flew toward the kitchen. "Give me an hour, and I will have a feast ready that's fit for a god."

Aidoneus and I laughed while his father scowled at the pixie. I'd take the levity after the day I'd had. There was a mountain still to climb, but I had my friends and family by my side. And my familiar back in my head. I couldn't ask for better Yule gifts.

CHAPTER 7

Thicket was shaking as he continued to work the silver into a shield. I felt awful for calling him back, but I really wanted to present Hades with the gifts. "Thank you for coming back. After the mess I presented, I really needed this to smooth things over with his dad."

Thicket paused with his tiny hands on the silver and looked up at me. "I would do anything for you, Phoebe. I left because Hades' power was overwhelming. I thought my wings were going to burn up. The entire mound is talking about how Thia lasted a couple of hours in his presence and made him food. No one's ever managed something so brave."

I picked up the dagger I retrieved from Aidoneus when Mythia went to cook dinner. I couldn't be in the same room as the god a second longer. Plus, I really did want to finish these gifts, but I no longer had my magic. Which meant I needed Thicket to do it for me.

"Nana was just as brave. She told him off." Nina was leaning forward in the chair next to Nana's recliner with a smile on her face.

Jean-Marc kept his gaze on the shield while he continued

manipulating the silver like Thicket had instructed. "It was freaking awesome. She put the god in his place, and Gammy showed him how much smarter she is than him."

"Hades is a father before he's a god," Nana blurted. "He came here as a dad concerned about his son and the woman he's chosen. Every parent is entitled to make sure their child's chosen partner is worthy. I simply had no patience for his continued tantrum. It wasn't a big deal."

Laughter burst from me, and I shook with the force of it. Nina and Jean-Marc joined in while Thicket looked at us like we had lost our minds. "You're lucky the god didn't unleash his full power and incinerate you on the spot. It speaks to how much he loves his son that he showed restraint."

"Honestly, I hadn't stopped to think about it," I admitted. "I was so bewildered and lost then flooded with emotion and memories after Aidoneus kissed me."

"So, he is your boyfriend, after all. And I can see he's joining us for the holidays." Jean-Marc gave me a shit-eating grin.

I chuckled and shook my head. "Like I told Hades. I hadn't labeled anything or even thought about how much I cared for him until his father tried to drive a wedge between us. In the face of Hades' derision, I wasn't about to fall prey to the old saying of not realizing what I had until it was gone. I suppose it was easier to recognize what had been building because I'd just gotten my memories and connections back."

Nina sighed and propped her head on her hand. "I hope I find a love like that someday."

"Don't settle for anything less. Either of you. Your great-grandfather and I shared a deep love. It's out there, but most go all in with the first good-looking guy or girl that comes along." I was surprised at Nana's warning. She never said anything like that to me. Of course, I wouldn't have listened when I met Miles. I was too enamored with the picture he'd painted me.

"Listen to Nana. She's wise beyond her years. On another note. Do you think we should add some runes to the dagger? It's stunning as it is, but I wonder if it's too plain for a god." I didn't want to insult Thicket, but I had to ask. He would be crushed if Hades said it was trash.

"That's why I was coming up earlier. I was about to add runes and wanted to know if I should spell it with strength, stealth, or lethality." I was relieved when there was no evidence in Thicket's voice of him being offended.

"Can we do all three?" I couldn't choose between them.

Thicket's eyes went wide as he looked up at me. "I can't possibly spell them with all three in the amount of time I have. I'm almost done with the dragon, but I need to do the shield's runes for protection and impenetrability. You can't make one without both."

Nina jumped to her feet. "Can I do one? I helped with the Hellmouth and think I can do this."

Thicket paused and considered my daughter. "We can try. It'll be easier for you since we have silver cords. That way, you can create the rune and cast it at the same time. Let me draw them. That way, you have an example to copy."

Nina was beaming, her joy undeniable. "I won't let you down, Thicket."

The tiny pixie flew to my daughter and laid a hand on her cheek. It was smaller than the mole she had above the left side of her lip. "I know you won't. After all, you've had the best teacher."

We all laughed at that as Thicket sketched the runes and told her what each stood for. I watched as she placed the dagger in the stand Thicket used to keep the weapons steady while he worked.

I grabbed the thin cord from the drawer and handed it to

my daughter, then stood close while she worked. Within moments Nana was snoring in her chair, and Nina had the tip of her tongue poking out the right side of her mouth.

Heat emanated from her fingertips as she applied the cord and shaped it to match the symbol. With each layer, she cast the spell that went with the rune. She was immersed in her work, as were Thicket and Jean-Marc, so none of them noticed the tears that burned in my eyes.

It hadn't been long, but I missed my magic. I should be helping her finish this gift, but I was impotent at the moment. Fury had me clenching my fists as I fought back my emotions. It didn't help that the man with the hammer was back inside my skull, making it ache.

Nina worked in silence for several long minutes. A bright spark emitted from the symbol while Nina worked, waking Nana up. "What happened? Are we being attacked?"

"Everything's fine, Nana," I assured her.

My grandmother got out of her chair and joined me at the table. "That's beautiful, Nina. You're a natural, just like your mom. You too, Jean-Marc."

"This is harder than it looks," my son admitted. "If Thicket wasn't so patient, I don't think I would have gotten the hang of it."

Jean-Marc straightened and considered the shield. "That's badass. Can you help me make one before I go back to school, Thicket?"

"I'd be honored to help." Thicket beamed at Jean-Marc, clearly meaning what he said.

"Alright. I think I got it. It's a little rough along the edges, but I can't smooth them out, and I'm afraid to ruin what I've done." Nina held the dagger up for us to see.

Thicket looked over from the shield and smiled. "Your Nana is right. You're a natural. You almost did it perfectly. There isn't much that needs to be touched up. Let me finish the last layer on the runes, and I will smooth the few areas that need it."

Thicket lifted the tiny tool and ran it along with the rune he'd been working on for the past few minutes. Jean-Marc had been finishing the gold of the dragon with a similar tool. It was designed for clay sculpting, but the pixie had adapted it for us by adding silicone to the tip to heat it and smooth the metal.

Mythia buzzed down the stairs and stopped at the bottom. "Dinner is ready."

My heart skipped a beat then started racing in my chest. The speed made me dizzy. Or maybe that was the throbbing in my head. "Thicket is almost done. We will be right there."

"We're eating in the formal dining room." Mythia took off before I could object. We never used the room. I had considered transforming it into a space for the pixie to sleep when she slept over but hadn't gotten around to it yet. Now, I was glad. Given Hades' initial reaction, formality was a better bet.

Less than a minute later, Thicket stopped and held the dagger up to me. I took it, loving what they had created. "This is perfect. I owe you more than you know for saving me with these."

Thicket's cheeks turned pink, and he lowered his head. "Wait until you see if the god likes them."

"His reaction doesn't matter, Thicket. What you and the kids made is absolutely perfect. I'll use them if he doesn't want them."

Nana laughed at me as she turned for the stairs. "That's the smartest thing I've heard all night. Now, let's go get some food. I'm hungry."

Jean-Marc picked up the shield, and I carried the dagger. Butterflies fluttered in my stomach as we made our way to the dining room. Layla and Tsekani had joined my mom, Aidoneus, and Hades for dinner.

I walked to the head of the table where the god was sitting and held the dagger out with both hands. "We wanted to give you this for Yule. I haven't had time to wrap it and wanted to give it to you before you have to return to the Underworld."

Hades gaped at me before he closed his mouth and reached out to take the dagger. He ran a finger down the sharp blade. "This is beautiful."

It was my turn to gape at the God of the Underworld. Jean-Marc nudged me aside and presented him with the shield. "We crafted this to go with it." My son set it on the table in front of the god.

It was then that I noticed the fine china and shiny silverware. Mythia had used chargers and enough cutlery at each place setting for everyone present. I always thought it was ridiculous to switch forks during a meal.

"I didn't expect gifts. It's a pleasant surprise. And this work rivals that of my good friend, Hephaestus. Thank you."

My heart was still beating hard enough to burst through my ribcage, but it didn't diminish the relief I felt. "You're welcome."

Aidoneus wrapped me in his arms and pressed a brief kiss to my lips. His eyes told me I'd done well. "Shall we eat? This food smells delicious."

I chuckled and patted his muscled stomach. "Sounds good to me. I'm starving."

Mythia and my mom brought dishes into the room and placed them on the table. My mom lifted the lid off the soup tureen and smiled at me. "I made you that street soup you love."

Nina clapped her hands. "And Panang curry?"

My mom chuckled and nodded. "Yes, there's curry. And, Pad Thai."

Hades remained quiet while everyone took seats. Nana

took the other head of the table and didn't bother waiting for him. Instead, she grabbed the closest dish and put some onto her plate.

For the next few minutes, the sound of cutlery scraping ceramic and appreciative humming filled the room. When all of our plates were filled, we dug in without delay. Nana was eating an eggroll when she addressed Hades.

"I've always wondered something, Hades. Are the rumors true? Did you force Persephone into mating with you? I worried that was something your son would do to my granddaughter until I got to know him."

I choked on some noodles and started coughing. "Nana!" Aidoneus patted my back, trying to dislodge the food stuck there.

Hades waved a hand while he chewed the bite of food in his mouth. "It's a valid question. One, I get a lot. But it isn't one I answer. I don't have to tell you about my relationship with my wife. That's between her and me."

Nana snorted and sneered at the God of the Underworld. "That's an admission if I ever heard one. I feel sorry for your son and his mother. I bet you don't bother hiding any affairs you may have, either. I'm glad I got to know Aidoneus before discovering this information. I might have misjudged him otherwise."

"This entire family is rude. I thought I was wrong when you presented me with such stunning gifts. It turns out I was right." Hades pushed his half-eaten food away.

"And, it's beyond rude to force women into relationships they don't want." Nana huffed and crossed her arms over her chest.

Aidoneus placed a hand on his father's shoulder. "Don't, father. There is no need to be obstinate with Phoebe or her family. Amelia was asking out of genuine curiosity. How many times have I explained the trouble the misinformation causes for others?"

Hades glared daggers at Nana. For a split second, his eyes glowed red, and I almost dove across the table to shield her from his attack. "I could kill Demeter for saying such blasphemous things."

Aidoneus sighed and ran a hand through his hair. "There's no need for that. Mom and I give her enough shit about it. To answer your question, Amelia. My mother was not forced into mating with my father."

"So why did her mother start such a nasty lie?" Nana asked around a mouthful of curry.

"I'd bet she was trying to split them up," I blurted, then cringed when Hades shifted his intense black gaze my way.

"I'm nothing like my mother-in-law. I would never try and come between two people in love." Hades grabbed his plate and resumed eating as if he hadn't been doing that very thing an hour ago.

For once that night, I managed to remain silent about the topic. Aidoneus, however, did not. "That's the kettle calling the pot black. You were trying to do that exact thing to Phoebe and me, father. The difference between you and my grandmother is that you backed down when you saw how much we care for each other."

"I was merely looking out for your well-being," Hades insisted. "It's different."

Nana rolled her eyes. "If that's not true, is it true your mother spends half the year in the Underworld and the other half with her mom on Olympus?"

"That's true." Hades' words were clipped as he shoveled a bite of curry and rice into his mouth.

Aidoneus placed a hand over his father's on the table. "My dad sacrificed a great deal to allow my mother to be with her mother half of the year. A mated god is extremely possessive and unpleasant when they have to be away from their true love match. And yet, my dad never asked my mom to choose between her mother and him. He struck a deal allowing her to spend time in both realms. Not many in his position would have done the same thing."

I thought about how happy I was that Aidoneus was here with me full-time and winced when I realized I didn't want him gone from me six months of the year. I should be more understanding about the fact that Hades wanted his son to be home. His wife was already gone half the time, and now one of his children wasn't there.

"It's a good thing Aidon can visit you often. I can only imagine how lonely it can be when she's gone." I rubbed a hand over my chest where an ache started just thinking about the prospect. I didn't know enough about Aidoneus's sister to know if she was in the Underworld or not.

"It's not easy for him to come home now." Hades was unable to hide the sadness in his voice.

"But it's not impossible," I pointed out. "I can help him pass through the Hellmouth if necessary."

Jean-Marc leaned on the table and looked down at Hades. "Is there cell reception in the Underworld?"

The God of the Underworld chuckled at the question. The movement sent his energy rolling through the room. It was slightly oppressive, but I didn't get the sense the God was trying to intimidate us. It seemed he wasn't aware of it half the time. "No. We don't have cell phones."

Nina cocked her head. "Then how do you communicate with each other? There must be a way for you to talk with one another."

"As father and son, we can communicate telepathically. It's easier for me to reach out to Aidoneus than it is for him to try and connect with me."

My jaw dropped open wide enough to fit a big-mouth

burger. Before I could respond to that tidbit of information, my phone rang. I jumped to my feet, not wanting to miss a call from Lilith.

I grabbed the cell from the desk and answered without looking at the screen. "Hey. Please tell me you have good news for me."

"I don't know that I'd call it good news," my ex-husband replied, making my blood freeze and my stomach knot up.

"What do you want?" I didn't take anything aside from my personal belongings and mementos from my children's lives when I left the house.

"I want to know why you refused to let me have the kids for the holidays. They haven't been home since you left me."

I growled hearing that asshat say I left him. That couldn't be farthest from the truth. I had been so pissed off at him for ruining twenty years of marriage. I let that go months ago when I realized he'd done me a favor. I wasn't thrilled with him. I spent all my time making sure he was happy that I never stopped to ask myself what I wanted.

I took a deep breath and let it out slowly. "I did no such thing. I would never keep the kids from you. You never called and asked them to go to your house. In fact, when was the last time you even called Nina?" I recalled Jean-Marc saying his father had called to tell him he needed to cut back on the money he gave him because he was paying me too much in child support.

Miles heaved one of his deep sighs. It was the sound he made when he was exasperated with me. "You can't keep them from me, Phoebe. They're my kids too, and I want them for Christmas. Send them down here."

"You can deflect all you want. I know you haven't called Nina since I discovered you sleeping with that *child*. And for the record, I never forced them to stay here for the holidays. It was their choice."

"But you can make them come down to my place. You have your mother and grandmother while I'm alone in our house without my family."

"And, whose fault is that?" I wanted to jump through the phone line and strangle the asshole. "Where's your little chickie? Did she get tired of being with an old man already?"

"Put Jean-Marc on the phone." Miles hadn't changed one bit. He was still ordering me around and dismissing everything I said.

I dropped the phone and walked back into the dining room. "Jean-Marc, Nina. Your father is on the phone. Do you want to talk to him?"

Both of my kids looked like deer caught in the headlights. I picked up my cell then hit the mute button, so Miles wouldn't hear this next part. "It's alright if you want to speak to him. You don't have to do anything you don't want to do. I will love and support you regardless of your decision, but I want you to remember he is still your father regardless of his faults. Just because I don't like the man doesn't mean you have to hate him, too."

Jean-Marc got up and hugged me tightly. "Thanks, mom." He took the phone, and Nina followed him out of the dining room after giving me a smile from the other side of the table.

I sank back into my chair and rubbed my temples to ward off the ache Miles had inspired. This pain was different from that caused by the curse. My heart was being squeezed by a vice. Miles had broken up with his girlfriend. Or she had called things quits. Either way, he would try and convince my kids to go spend the holidays with him. I would support whatever decision they made, regardless of how painful it might be.

"Would you like me to discover who is behind the curse, Phoebe?"

My eyes snapped open at the question from the God of

the Underworld. I stared at Hades, completely baffled as to why he was offering to help me. He'd said nothing for the past few moments. I assumed he couldn't do anything for me. Why was he offering now? I was half-convinced he was messing with me by asking. That was how my day had been going so far.

CHAPTER 8

Everyone at the table was silent as a tomb. No one spoke. No one moved. I doubted anyone was even breathing. I, for one, was holding my breath for fear of breaking the spell. Hades had just offered me a lifeline. One I desperately needed.

"Why would you help me? More importantly. What will it cost me? My soul?"

Hades threw back his head and laughed. The sound shook the walls and rattled the windows. "You like playing with your life, don't you, little witch?"

Next to me, Aidoneus chuckled as he squeezed my hand under the table. "You just can't help yourself, can you, father?"

Hades looked at his son with one brow lifted. "On the contrary, son. I'm impressed with the woman you've chosen. She's smart for having lived a life as a mundane. Of course, it's not all that surprising given her family."

I took that as a compliment to my mother and Nana. They'd always been my guiding light. There weren't better examples of strength in the world. Because of them, I didn't fall apart when I discovered Miles's affair. They stood by me when I was forced to move back home with my mom and Nana.

"But to answer your question, Phoebe. This will cost you nothing. It's enough that you care for my son and will not stand in the way of him visiting home as often as necessary." Hades' explanation confirmed my earlier suspicion. The god was lonely. He missed his family.

I looked at Aidoneus for confirmation that I could trust his father's offer. It was Tarja that answered instead. *"The god's word is binding. He cannot ask for something in return for this favor. Such an offer is rare. You can trust him in this."*

"That's what I needed to know. I'm glad to have you back. Even if I can barely hear you and can't feel you, I know you are there for me." I held my familiar's gaze for a second longer then turned to Hades.

"If that's the case, then I would love your help. How do we go about getting these answers?" I pushed my plate away and rested my arms on the table.

Hades leaned back in his chair and ran a hand along his jaw. "I'll need a few supplies." His gaze shifted around the room, and one corner of his mouth lifted briefly. "Although I'm not sure you will have what I need."

I restrained from rolling my eyes. "Whatever it is, I will get it. Unless, of course, it can only be found in another realm."

The God of the Underworld looked from me to my familiar. "I'll need the soul of a familiar from Stuleros and some single malt scotch. And a creme brulee so I can do the spell."

Shock traveled through me. Not about the scotch or dessert, but about the soul of a familiar. "I'm not certain we can get the soul of a familiar."

"It won't be possible to travel to my realm with Phoebe's magic

blocked. I'll be attacked if I travel there alone. You will have to use my soul."

My heart hammered in my chest at the same time a vice closed around it. "No. I won't risk your safety just to get answers. I can't risk losing you, Tarja."

Mythia hovered above the spot she had been sitting and eating and held up a hand. "While you guys discuss what you will do, I'll get the scotch and crème brulee."

I nodded my head. "Thanks, Thia."

"Phoebe, we need to have Hades use me," Tarja insisted. Her voice was a mere whisper in my mind, but there was no missing the determination in hers. *"Now that I have a pathway into your mind, I can feel the energy building. We won't have more than a couple days to get the answers we need. I would rather risk my life than take a chance of you having your brain melted. Nina isn't ready to inherit the crown. It would make her a bigger target than you."*

I took a deep breath and closed my eyes to hide the tears gathering there. Some part of me knew I didn't have long. The pain grew by the minute. It was only a matter of minutes before my mind went fuzzy again.

Opening my eyes, I inclined my head to her. "Alright. We use Tarja. How does this work?"

Mythia flew in carrying a silver tray, followed by my mom. I hadn't seen her get up to help the pixie. My mom set the much larger platter on the table. She put a ramekin of fruit topped dessert in front of Hades while Mythia set a crystal decanter and whiskey glass in front of the god.

Hades removed the glass stopper and poured himself several fingers of the amber liquid. "That's the best choice you could have made in this difficult situation. I would have gone into Stuleros myself, but the gods were banned millennia ago by the Pleiades."

Beside me, Aidoneus's grip tightened on my hand. It was

a silent message not to ask what happened. I returned the gesture letting him know I understood. "What do you need me to do?"

"Change seats with my son, then clear your mind. And don't react, no matter what you hear or see. If you break my concentration in the middle of this process, your house may not survive the process." Hades was nice by saying my house might not survive when I knew the people inside were at more risk than the building.

Aidoneus pressed a chaste kiss to my lips as we both stood up. I wanted to sink into his lips and lose myself in the passion always brewing between the two of us. Instead, I took his seat and clasped my hands in my lap.

Hades took a sip of the scotch then twirled a finger in Tarja's direction. Her body floated to the table where he deposited her. She yowled at him, and I swear she added a glare, too.

Hades chuckled and took a bite of the dessert. "Mmmm. This is delicious. It was meant to coax the soul to cooperate with the process, but if you don't need it, I will eat it."

Tarja snagged the rim with one claw and yanked the dessert to her. Before she could dig in, her back arched, and she let out a howl that made the hair on the back of my neck stand on end.

She twisted and arched. I moved to reach for her, but my hands flew to the sides of my head instead. Sharp pain sliced through my neural pathways as pressure built inside my skull. Blood dripped from my nose onto the table in front of me.

I was helpless in the face of my pain while Tarja's body went limp and her chest rattled with every breath. The sound froze my blood. It was the death rattle. I'd heard it countless times in dying patients at the hospital and would never forget it.

When her chest went still, a bluish version of Tarja drifted up from her body. It was a lot like a ghost. Speaking of specters, Evanora hovered in the corner, concern etched across her features.

Tarja's spirit hissed at Hades before she settled next to me. The second her ghostly paw touched my arm, the pain vanished, leaving me gasping for breath. I was so freaking done with this curse bullshit. I should have been used to hurting, but I wasn't. I preferred to avoid it whenever possible.

Hades chanted under his breath, his hands glowing where they hovered on either side of Tarja and me. The dessert caught Tarja's attention, and her spirit was trying to move closer to her. Smiling, I moved it to her without breaking contact.

She lapped at the crème and fruit, oblivious to the fact that she couldn't actually eat anything. The light from Hades surrounded us both then sunk into my chest. The sensation was warm and seeking. It touched on an excruciating part, stealing my breath.

Thankfully, the discomfort was short-lived. Hades lowered his hands, and his light vanished. Tarja's spirit floated back to her body and sunk inside. She instantly jumped to her feet and hissed at the God of the Underworld.

"You could have warned me it was going to be painful for Phoebe. I almost fought you." I'd never heard Tarja so pissed before.

Hades shrugged his shoulders and downed the glass of scotch. "Eat the sugar. You'll need it."

Tarja's back arched, but she ultimately dove into the dessert with relish. *"So, what did you learn? Who is responsible?"*

Rather than answer Tarja, Hades shifted his gaze to Tsekani. "Are you sure you want the answer?"

I slapped the top of the table to get his attention. "I'm positive! I'm dying here and refuse to go out without a fight."

"I know you want the information. I'm asking Tsekani if he wants to know." Unease rippled through me with the god's reply.

He would only address my friend about this because he wasn't going to like the answer. I was torn about forcing the information to come to light. On the one hand, I wanted to protect Tsekani from being hurt. On the other, I *had* to get the details to save my life.

Tsekani's face paled, and he clasped his hands on the tabletop. "I'm certain. Nothing matters more than protecting Phoebe and removing this curse."

"Keep that conviction close to heart," Hades advised the dragon shifter. "Brody is behind the curse on Phoebe."

"That's not possible," Tsekani insists. "Brody is a shifter. He can't cast spells, let alone curse someone. Besides, he knows how much Phoebe means to me. He would never hurt her like that."

The tension in the room was electric, like a bomb about to explode. Aidoneus was the one to light the fuse as he burst out of his chair. "Did you know?" My boyfriend was in Tsekani's face and dragging him to his feet and shoving him against the wall.

I grabbed Aidon's arm and tried to pry him away from Tsekani. "Stop. Tsekani wouldn't keep this from us. He didn't know." Aidon let go and wrapped his arms around me.

Hades answered as if his son hadn't just attacked Tsekani. "Brody did not create the curse, but he helped the young man deliver the charm to Phoebe. He is the one that has the rest of the answers you need."

"We need to talk to him. Get him here now." Nana's demand brokered no other option.

Tsekani sank to the floor, his eyes bright with betrayal

and his head in his hands. "I'll ask him to come over. I can't believe he did this to us. Why?"

I crouched in front of him and rested a hand on his knee. "He's the only one that can tell us. I'm sorry this happened. I wish I could change the details, so it was someone else."

Tsekani took his cell phone out and typed a message. He paused at one point, then growled and tapped some more. I wanted to lean over and look at what he wrote but refrained.

When Tseki met my gaze a second later, I saw raw determination along with anger and betrayal. "I will get the answers from him. I promise you I won't let him keep it from us. I'm sorry for bringing him into this house."

"None of this is your fault, Tsekani. I know this must be difficult for you. I'm here for you whatever you need," I promised him.

Nina joined us. "We all are."

Things were looking up for me for the first time in what felt like the longest day in history. We would break this curse and have a great holiday season together. Well, most of us. My gut churned when I looked at the despair in Tsekani's eyes. I just hoped this didn't destroy my warm-hearted friend.

* * *

"Hey, Brody. Nice to see you again." It took great effort to keep from throttling the guy when I opened the door, especially with how pissed I still was after Miles called.

Aidoneus was bristling behind me. His anger was enough to scald my senses. I stepped aside and grabbed Aidon's hand with a smile.

Brody entered the house while he scanned me head to toe. "How are you doing, Phoebe?"

I would have dismissed his question before. Now I know

it betrayed his true agenda. "Great, actually. I was a nervous wreck about Aidon's dad visiting, but it's turned out okay."

Brody's eyes widened, and he looked around then back at the door just as Aidoneus was shutting it. Aidon gave him a tight smile. "Hades is here?" Brody's voice held a definite note of strain.

Tsekani came out of the formal dining room in a rush of cologne and all smiles. The dragon shifter was a good-looking guy in his silk shirt and dress pants. "Hello, love. Miss me?"

To Tseki's credit, he only hesitated a brief second before embracing his boyfriend and kissed him on the lips. Aidon and I continued to the dining room to keep up appearances, where we resumed our seats.

Hades had a grin on his face as he sipped his fourth glass of scotch. We all remained silent while we waited for the couple to join us. Brody's dark skin lost all color a few seconds later as he entered the room holding hands with Tsekani. He paused near the exit and tugged on Tseki's hand.

Tsekani released Brody and crossed his arms over his chest. "What's wrong, Brody?"

I almost felt bad when sweat broke out across Brody's forehead. "No...nothing. I didn't realize we were going to have dinner with everyone, is all."

Selene approached from behind the shifter along with Layla. We'd planned to box him in once he got into the room. If he had the chance, there was no doubt the guy would try and flee.

"I wanted to have a chat with you," Aidoneus told him as he got up and prowled around the table. "You see, my father gave us some interesting information."

Brody swallowed and shoved his shaking hands in his pockets. "What did he say?" I thought the guy would pass out when his eyes traveled to the god enjoying his scotch.

Aidon cracked his knuckles. "He told us how you conspired to curse Phoebe. What I want to know is who you are working with and why you would betray your boyfriend like that." I allowed Aidoneus to take the lead. I was liable to bite his head off without getting answers. My blood was still boiling after having to talk to Miles earlier.

Brody flinched and lifted his hands in the air. "Apparently, it didn't work. Phoebe is fine. Can't we just put this behind us?"

Aidoneus went to grab Brody, but his body flew into the wall and slid toward the ceiling by several feet. He dangled there gasping while all eyes shifted to the God of the Underworld, where he was pointing at Brody with a glowing finger.

Aidoneus growled and clenched his hands into fists. "I wanted to wrap my hands around his throat, father."

"I know, son, but if I allowed that, Brody would be dead right now. This way, he will answer your questions," Hades replied. His words held power that reverberated through the room and slammed into Brody's chest.

Nana arched a brow and gestured to Brody. "He can't do that if he can't breathe, Hades."

"Good point, Amelia." The sound of gasping told us Hades had loosened his hold, although Brody's body didn't move an inch. "Answer my son."

Brody had tears in his eyes when he looked at Tsekani. The defeat was etched into his features. "I found the mage to deliver the curse. He lived one town over and was easily manipulated after she took his wife hostage."

Tsekani's following scream held every ounce of hurt and betrayal he felt. "Why would you do that?"

The tears fell down Brody's cheeks. "Because she doesn't appreciate you enough. She gives you menial tasks and expects you will follow her like her slave. It's not your job to do her dirty work."

Tsekani slammed a fist into the wall next to Brody's body. "It's my fucking job to protect her. She's never taken me for granted and never seen me like a slave. She's one of my closest friends."

Brody snarled and partially shifted, fighting against the invisible hold on him. His teeth turned to sharp canines and fur-covered his arms. Spit dribbled down his chin, and he thrashed his head from side to side.

Aidoneus came to stand behind my chair and put his hands on the back of it. "This woman would die for any of her friends. You fucked up by making an enemy of her, Brody. If you're lucky, all she will do is banish you from her territory. If I'm lucky, she will let me skin you alive. I want the name of the witch that roped you into this scheme."

"The decision of what happens to you is up to Tsekani," I interjected. I would never make this decision when I wasn't the one really hurt by his actions. Tsekani was the one betrayed, not me. "But if he isn't able to, I'm inclined to give Aidon what he wants."

Hades chuckled. "I like how blood-thirsty she is."

It was a wonder Brody hadn't peed himself yet. He was now shaking with fear rather than trying to escape. "It was a witch named Nissa. She promised me you would lose your mind before being unable to continue with your role as Hattie's heir. You were supposed to be freed."

Scales rippled over Tsekani's skin, and his eyes shifted to a slitted pupil. "There was no need to free me. I want to be here with her. I'm bound by my word and my desire. Nothing more."

"Underestimating Phoebe was a mistake," Hades announced as he got to his feet. "One you and this Nissa will regret as long, or short, as you live. If you both had your way, the world would have been thrown into chaos. You're lucky she's strong enough to combat some of this curse. If my son had lost her, his plans would look like child's play next to what I would do to you."

My head was spinning. Seriously it was like being on a roller coaster without breaks or an end. The night started with Hades hating me and ended with him backing me. It was an issue to think about another time. Right now, we had a witch named Nissa to find.

CHAPTER 9

Lilith kept glancing over her shoulder and trying to get a glimpse of Hades, where he was standing near the back door. Nana was next to him, talking about god knows what. I would have intervened and tried to keep her from him, but Nana had earned Hades's respect.

"The *actual* God of the Underworld is in your house, Phoebe!" Lilith's voice was practically a hiss in my ear.

I smiled and patted her shoulder. "I know. He's Aidoneus's father and came for the holidays."

Lilith turned back to the computer and resumed her typing. "Your life is frightening. How do you handle it with such grace? I'd be a terrible wreck if I were you. I mean, you're cursed and in danger of having your mind melted, and you have a powerful god in your home. Oh, and then there is the betrayal of one of your own."

My head throbbed with each new fact she ticked off. "That's nothing compared to my ex-husband. Not killing him was the real challenge. Have you discovered who this Nissa Quinn is yet?"

Lilith clicked a document and pulled up what looked like a spreadsheet of employee names. There were tabs at the bottom for each of the companies under the Silva Corp umbrella. I tried to scan the words but didn't get far when it shifted and highlighted a name.

"Who's Morgan Quinn? Do you know her? I don't recall passing her up for promotion." My brain hurt, and there were too many decisions I made with Lilith to recall the witch.

Lilith wrote something on a sticky note, and I didn't expect her to respond right away, but she did. "Morgan is one of the employees at the warehouse where we store the products from Glaziarts. She applied for a promotion when Glen left, but we decided another employee was a better match for the position."

"We as in you and me? Because it seems her daughter is blaming me for this decision. She convinced Brody to help her put a Blood curse on me. Does that make her Tainted now?" I hadn't considered the question until now.

Lilith pushed away from the small desk and stood up. "It was you and I. She had applied to be the Project Manager for the delivery trucks. She'd been Glen's Executive Assistant for decades. She knew the process, but she didn't have a degree like the candidate we ended up hiring. And, no. She isn't Tainted. She never used Dark magic to steal someone's power."

"I don't understand. She cursed me. That seems pretty freaking dark if you ask me." I wanted her to be Tainted because it would make it easier to hate her. The girl was avenging her mother. Part of me admired her love and devotion.

"Cursing someone is slimy and underhanded, but it isn't Dark magic. She used her blood during the creation, making it impossible for another to break what she created without her. She was definitely walking a fine line. I find that those willing to go to this length aren't far from falling from the tree entirely." Lilith's words sent a chill through me.

"After I find her, we need to do whatever it takes to bring her back from the edge. I don't want her to go dark because she loved her mother."

Lilith's shallow gasp echoed in the suddenly silent kitchen. "You've proven yourself to be a worthy heir, Phoebe. I had my doubts at first, but it takes an extraordinary person to look past what was done to them and to the well-being of the one that attacked."

That was the nurse in me. I was built to help others. And I was who I was because of the love and guidance of my mom and grandmother.

Aidoneus grabbed the keys from the desk and jingled them in his hand. "Don't give her too much credit, Queenie. She hasn't removed the curse yet. Dig into that bloodthirsty woman you displayed an hour ago."

Tsekani extended his hand to Lilith. She placed the address in his palm. "Let's get this handled. I want Brody gone as soon as possible."

"I can take him to the Underworld with me," Hades offered. "I have plenty to keep him occupied while you're deciding what to do with him."

Tsekani sucked in a breath and lowered his head. I saw the tears he was fighting to keep from falling. I smiled at the God of the Underworld. "I appreciate the offer, but I think we will pass. If Tsekani changes his mind, I'll have Aidoneus let you know."

Hades inclined his head then crossed to his son. He pulled him into a warm hug and held on for several seconds. "I'm going to return home. I expect to see you soon."

Aidon chuckled. "Yes, sir. I promise to visit within the

next two weeks. Thank you for helping Phoebe. You saved her life. Brody is the last place we would have looked."

I extended my hand to Hades. "It was wonderful to meet you. I would say I owe you for what you did, but Tarja assures me that's not a good idea."

A bolt of energy zapped me when the god clasped my hand. He was dampening his power. I felt how much effort he was pouring into blocking his signal, but he couldn't contain it all. I shook my hand out when he released me.

"The trip wasn't wasted. My son might not be moving home, but he is happy, and I was given a priceless gift." Hades gestured to the shield and dagger with his chin.

"Can you do me a favor?" I hope Hades doesn't laugh at me for this one. "Can you extend an invitation to Fate? I would like to invite her over for wine Wednesdays."

Hades blinked at me for a second before he chuckled. "You never cease to surprise me. Which one?"

I cocked my head to the side and considered what I knew about Greek mythology. "I suppose all three, seeing as they've all been playing with the strings of my life."

Hades' eyes darkened as he looked from his son to me. "I'd be happy to extend the invitation. It would do them good to reconnect with humanity. They've lost perspective over the centuries hiding in their cave."

I swallowed my retraction. What the heck had I gotten myself into now? No way was I backing down. I really wanted to get these sisters on my good side. "Thank you."

The god inclined his head then returned to the door to say goodbye to Nana while I turned to Lilith, who was standing there gaping at us. Leaning toward her, I murmured, "You might want to close your mouth. Thank you for coming on short notice and helping find Nissa."

She snapped her jaw closed. "Anytime. Let me know if I can help."

I nodded my head and followed Aidoneus to the front door. My head felt like it had been turned into a milkshake, but my hope surpassed it all. I was going to lift this curse, and the visit with Hades was done. Yule with my kids was going to be picture perfect. Unless they were planning to head to their father's house.

Don't borrow more problems than you need to. Right. I'd deal with that after I was cleared.

AIDONEUS PULLED up to a house not far from Marilee's Bakery. It was a two-story white Cape Cod style with a slate-grey roof. The yard was well kept, and the place looked like it was in good shape. This was the type of neighborhood I'd lived in my whole life.

"Brody lives three houses down."

I looked back at Tsekani and saw him pointing to a light grey house not far from where we were parked. That explained how they knew each other. I reached back and squeezed his hand. "I'm sorry, Tseki. You don't have to do this, you know. Aidoneus and I can handle this on our own."

"I'm going inside. I will protect you until you this is done. Brody asked me to meet up with him earlier tonight because he planned this to happen. The date was a ploy to get me out of the house so I wouldn't sniff the curse. If I was there, I wouldn't have missed it. I'd bet money he had Layla called away as well. Her nose is even better than mine."

"Stop beating yourself up, man. There is nothing you can do except to help Phoebe with the reversal. You didn't make the unfortunate choice. Brody did. You ready to go inside?" I fell more in love with Aidoneus as he tried to reassure my friend. He was definitely one of the good ones.

Tsekani nodded and climbed out of the car. Aidon and I

joined him on the sidewalk. My heart began racing as we approached. My anger rose above my discomfort the closer we got.

Aidoneus angled his body, so I was behind him and knocked on the door. A young woman with light brown hair and hazel eyes opened the door. She was short, barely five feet tall, and was dressed in an ugly Christmas sweater.

"Are you Nissa?"

The young woman smiled and cocked one hip out. "I am. Who's asking?"

"I'm Aidoneus. Son of Hades. I'm here to talk to you about Phoebe Dieudonne`." Nissa's eyes went wide, and she tried to slam the door shut. Aidon stepped forward and thrust his hand out, stopping the panel from closing. Nissa automatically took a step backward.

I followed him inside and smiled at the young witch. "Hello, Nissa. I've been looking for you."

Her eyes narrowed on me, then traveled to Tsekani behind me. She lost more of her coloring and started wringing her hands together. "Why are you here?"

Aidoneus scoffed. "I'm certain you know precisely why we're here."

Tsekani spread his legs and crossed his arms over his chest. His anger was getting the better of him, and his pupils were slit while green scales covered his arms. He was a terrifying sight. Particularly when coupled with the sharp edges of Aidon's energy.

"Who's here, Niss?" An older woman walked into the room and stopped short when she saw us. Electricity crackled across her knuckles, making my hackles rise. This could get ugly fast.

"I wouldn't do that if I were you," Aidon warned. "We're here to talk to your daughter about removing a curse. I'd hate to have to hurt you in the process. From what I understand, you're innocent."

Nissa's mother flared her fingers, making the energy crackle. "Who do you think you are coming into my home like this? My daughter knows nothing about a curse."

Nissa grabbed her mom's hand. "Mom, don't. He's the son of Hades."

"You're Morgan Quinn, correct?" I asked, interrupting any further discussion. They both feared Aidoneus, which was to our benefit.

"Yes, I am." Her eyes narrowed as she looked at me closer. "You're Hattie's heir. What can I do for you?"

"You can tell your daughter to lift the Blood curse she cast on me."

Morgan flinched and shot wide-eyes to her daughter. "What is she talking about?"

Nissa burst into tears. "I had to do something, mom. They passed you up for someone that didn't know shit about the warehouse or the process. You had to train him."

Morgan gasped, and her hands flew to her mouth. "That does not mean you should curse people. She did what she believed was best for the company, honey. A Blood curse?" I heard the concern and fear in her voice. She was terrified her daughter was in danger of Turning.

"But you've worked so hard and have taken care of me by yourself ever since dad left ten years ago. You deserved more. I figured with her out of the way, Lilith would give you the raise you earned." Nissa grabbed her mom's hands and pleaded with her to understand.

"I can't believe you would do something like this. You should have left this alone. Using blood magic and curses are one step away from becoming Tainted." The mother's warnings were dire and seemed to reach Nissa.

"I'm so sorry. I would never go that far. You have to believe me."

"You can earn your mother's trust back by undoing the curse," Aidoneus barked. There wasn't a hint of understanding in his voice.

"She will," Morgan promised. "What spell did you use, Niss?"

"I used the binding curse and added confusion to the mix."

Morgan's head reared back. "How did you get ahold of her hair for the binding? Tell me you didn't break into her house, too. Goddess. I'll be lucky to come out of this with a job at all. What the hell were you thinking?"

Nissa's lower lip wobbled, and more tears streamed from her eyes. "Brody brought them to me. He said he got them from her brush."

Tsekani growled and started shifting. His arm muscles bulged, and his shirt ripped. Aidoneus jumped to his side and gripped his shoulders. "Not here. You need to calm down, or you are going to hurt Phoebe."

Tsekani inclined his head and took several deep breaths. His body shrank, but the scales remained. "I'm good." Aidon held him for another minute before turning back to us.

Morgan grabbed Nissa's arm and pulled her down the hall. We followed and found ourselves in an open floorplan living room and kitchen. "We are undoing this now."

Nissa nodded, went to an armoire, and grabbed a cauldron from the cupboard while her mother approached me. "We will need some of your hair to undo what my misguided daughter has done."

I tilted my head to focus on Aidoneus. "Is that how this works?"

"If she used hair to bind you, then she will need some to release you," he confirmed.

Morgan handed me a pair of scissors, and I clipped a few strands, handing them over. We watched as they dropped herbs, distilled water, and my hair into the cauldron. Rose quartz followed, and they cast a fire under the basin. They chanted about cleansing my energy.

Smoke drifted up from the cauldron as Morgan stirred the ingredients with magic using her finger. "Now, Nissa." At her mother's command, she pricked her finger and dropped blood into the pot. The mixture sizzled and sparked.

Nissa trained her gaze on me. *"Absolvisti, et dimiserunt ire."*

Fire exploded in my chest at the exact moment white light shot out of the pot and into me. Rather than intensifying the heat, it quelled it. A second later, a heavyweight was lifted from me, and I felt my magic churning.

Fire burst over my hands, and Tarja was back. I felt her. Better yet, I heard her loud and clear when she called out to me. *"I'm fine. I hear you. We did it. The curse is gone."*

"Thank the gods," Tarja replied. *"We will catch up when you get home."*

"Did it work?" Aidoneus asked. He was a couple inches from me with a pinched brow.

I took a deep breath, happy to have the agony in my skull and body gone. "It did. My magic is back, and better yet, Tarja is too." I conjured my witch fire and tossed the purple flames from palm to palm.

"Let's talk," I told Morgan and Nissa.

Nissa fell to her knees. "Don't punish my mom. She had nothing to do with this. It was all my fault."

The room was suddenly filled with black light, and the oxygen was being sucked from the room as Aidoneus grew in size and his eyes blazed red. "You almost killed the woman I love, and you're asking for mercy?"

I ignored the burning in my chest and placed my hands on the lower part of Aidon's chest. It was all I could reach now that the top of his head hit the ceiling. "Stop. We aren't hurting her. And you're taking all the air."

He returned to average size, and my next breath didn't hurt as much. "My control snapped the second I knew you were alright. I will follow your lead on this, love. But there will be no second chances. She needs to know that now."

I ran my hand over his heart, and his muscle jumped at my touch. "I agree. This is her one opportunity to be better."

Certain he wouldn't explode again, I turned to face Nissa and her mother. Nissa was still on her knees, and I was reasonably certain she was kneeling in a puddle of her own urine. Not that I blamed her. Aidon was terrifying a moment ago.

Not that it stopped me from salivating over the god. Seeing him so angry and ready to destroy to avenge me was hot as hell. Yeah, I was twisted, but then we already knew that.

"Morgan, you aren't losing your job. Far from it." I had to reassure her before I said anything else. I saw the resignation in her eyes and hated seeing it. She had done nothing but care for her daughter.

It wasn't easy being a single parent. You had to be both mother and father, and there was no one there to help with the hard stuff. Everything from injuries to broken hearts was on your shoulders. I'd watched my best friend, Fiona, do it for years and knew how demanding it was.

"Until we can find a new position for you, I am giving you a raise. It will be reflected in your next paycheck. But I want you to compile a list of jobs you think you would be good at and positions you would like to be considered for, and I will look it over."

Morgan's lower jaw dropped open, and she sputtered. "Why would you do this after what Nissa did?"

I shrugged my shoulders. "Her motives touched me. She

didn't attack me because she wanted my power. She did what she did to get you what you deserved. And she is right. Your hard work should be recognized and awarded."

"I don't even know what to say. I won't let you down. And neither will Nissa. I know you have to punish her. But please don't banish her. I would hate to have to leave Camden with her." It wasn't surprising that mom was willing to leave with her child. They obviously had a close bond.

"I'm not banishing her. I'm giving her a job."

"Because she's a good person," Tsekani blurted. No doubt anticipating their next question. "Much better than any of us."

I gave him a smile. "You're one of the best of us too, Tseki. The job has crap pay and focuses on coping mechanisms. The fact that you let yourself stew in anger until you resorted to questionable means is troubling, Nissa."

Aidon snorted. "That's an understatement. I know my Queenie believes you can be saved. I'm not so sure, so I will be waiting and watching."

I glared at Aidoneus. "That won't be necessary because if Nissa Turns, I will kill her. If she shows signs of worsening behavior and darker magic, I will imprison her. This is the only warning you will receive. I do believe you can find a better path, Nissa. With guidance and options, there should never be another situation to warrant resorting to Dark magic."

Morgan collapsed beside her daughter and wrapped her arms around her. Nissa looked up at me through her lashes. "I completely misjudged you, and for that, I am sorry. You're right that I allowed my anger to get the best of me. I will not let my mother down."

I smiled for real this time. "That's what I'm counting on."

It wasn't going to be the thought of being banished or killed that would get to her. She resorted to Blood magic for her mother. It wasn't until she saw her mother's disappointment and horror that the reality fully sank into her heart. There was nothing she wouldn't do for the woman that raised her, and that included being the best-behaved witch possible.

CHAPTER 10

Jean-Marc stood in the living room looking at me with his hands on his hips and a deep furrow between his eyes. "You gave her a job? She cursed you and almost killed you! You'd ground me for texting after ten at night, and she gets a job."

I set my mug of cocoa down on the coffee table. "It was a risk, I know. She did it for her mom, not from a desire for power. That matters. Plus, I'll be able to keep a closer eye on her through Lilith and Clio. And if I can give her a greater purpose as well as teach her coping mechanisms, then we've all won. We can't afford even one more Tainted witch in the world. Besides, it's the holidays. I'm feeling generous. It's the season of giving, right?"

Aidoneus bent and kissed the top of my head. "And that's yet another thing I love about you so much. I couldn't see past my anger and would have hurt her or worse if you hadn't intervened."

Tsekani released a heavy breath and gestured with his bottle of beer. "Me too. I was so pissed at Brody for taking action against you, yet I still love him and saw her as a scapegoat for that rage. I was a heartbeat from joining Aidon."

Nina wrapped an arm around Tseki's waist. She was short compared to him, and the top of her head came up to his armpit. "What are you going to do about him?"

Tsekani looked at me. The green scales remained on his arms, and his eyes were that of his dragon, telling me he was still distraught over this matter. I wanted to make this decision for him and save him some heartache, but I knew better than that. He would only have closure if he made a decision about what he wanted to happen to Brody.

After a few seconds, Tseki returned Nina's embrace. "Part of me wants to throw him into a version of Phoebe's rehab program, but I know better. He's not a young man, acting out of loyalty to me like Nissa. He knows better. Not to mention we have had several conversations about the fact that I was here because I wanted to be. He's always been jealous of the connection I formed with you from the first day we met. That's what this boils down to with him."

Jealousy was an ugly emotion. One that formed when one person cared deeply for another. It made me rethink banning Brody. He loved Tsekani, and I didn't blame him. The dragon shifter was intelligent, funny, and good-looking.

"I wouldn't be too harsh on him. It sounds like he doesn't see himself as good enough for you," my mom interjected. "That kind of insecurity usually comes from being taught you have to do more and be more at a young age."

"You're right. I know he loves me. Deep down, I don't think he's a bad guy, but I can never trust him again. Insecurity like that isn't justification for nearly causing someone's death. Perhaps if his reasoning wasn't so selfish, I would be able to ask for leniency. Is there a way you can make him do crappy work for free while he's under supervision? And make it so he can't leave his house and do whatever he wants? I don't want him sent to the Obsidian Tower or anything," Tsekani said.

"What's the Obsidian Tower?" I hadn't heard that term before.

"It's the paranormal prison. Once there, it's impossible to escape, and conditions are said to drive the magically inclined insane. Witches and mages lose their minds with the binds on their powers. It's similar to your curse, but for them, it is not lifted. It can't be because they could use magic to get out, so being sent there for many is a death sentence."

I gaped at my familiar. That sounded unpleasant. "We can develop a house arrest system for Brody. I wish I still worked at a hospital. Having him clean out bedpans would be unpleasant."

Tsekani laughed. "Especially, with his sensitive shifter nose."

"You can have him volunteer to do that," Nana pointed out. "First order of business is to make sure he can't leave his house and do something even dumber. We wouldn't want him to lash out because he feels threatened."

Aidoneus chuckled. "My father has him for now. We can deal with it after the holidays. I think we've all earned a few happy days."

Jean-Marc's face fell. "I'd love that, but Nina and I are going to visit dad in the morning. I was hoping we could have our family celebration tonight."

Emotion filled my chest, starting with anger. I couldn't believe Miles would pull that shit after everything he had done this past year. I held it back because I would never put my kids in a position to choose between their father and me.

"Good thing I've finished my shopping. Let's head into the kitchen to make the traditional Yule log cake. We never open presents without one."

Nina grabbed Tsekani's hand and tugged him out of the room. "You're going to love this."

"What is it?" The dragon shifter asked. I was happy to hear some of the emotion in his voice had lightened.

'It's a thin chocolate cake rolled like a log. It's got frosting inside. Gammy used to make the top look like an actual log for the fire," Nina explained.

My mom was smiling as she heard my daughter boast about her Yule Log. "That takes an eternity, or I would do it for you guys tonight. Why don't you bring the presents into the kitchen, Phoebe? That way, we can cook and open then eat."

"Good idea, mom." Instead of following everyone out, I went to the tree in the living room and grabbed the packages from underneath.

Aidoneus and Layla had followed me, and they helped carry the presents into the kitchen. Mythia and Mom had the counter covered with ingredients and the mixer by the time we entered.

I set my load on the island, and so did the others. Selene was hanging back by the arch and looked like she would retreat upstairs to her bedroom.

Grabbing one of the packages, I handed Selene the gift I'd gotten her for Yule. "This is part of your gift. The other part is my promise to make finding a solution for your situation a priority. No more putting all the other visitor's problems first. We are going to figure out how to get your spirit back into your body so you can leave the house and live a full life without worry about being possessed again."

Tears spilled down the ghoul's cheeks, and she threw her arms around my neck and hugged me close. "Thank you, thank you, thank you, Phoebe. You have so many things happening in your life that I never expected my issues to take precedence. The other's matter, too."

Nana patted the girl on the back, making Selene release me. "Of course, the others are important. But we don't let family suffer if there's something we can do about it, child."

"I'm family?" The vulnerability in Selene's eyes was heart-wrenching.

My mom jumped into the conversation and wrapped an arm around Selene's shoulders. "You became a member the second you walked through the door."

Evanora floated closer. "She's right. I could see them embrace you right away. It's what gave me the courage to finally speak up. I knew they'd accept me, too."

"It's my fault for not addressing you earlier," I admitted to Evanora, our resident ghost. "I thought I was losing my mind the times I caught sight of you. When I asked Hattie, and she said you were upset because I wasn't paying attention to you, I even considered getting her an MRI and other tests to check for dementia."

Everyone laughed at that. *"I told Hattie we needed to let you in on the secret before you ran away screaming. She said we had to wait for the right moment."*

I looked to my familiar. "Do you think she sensed what was going to happen? If I left earlier and hadn't intervened with Myrna, I wouldn't be here today."

"Yes. I'm sure Hattie was aware she had less time than I assumed. She wanted you to take her place, and as usual, she was right. There isn't another person better suited to be the Pleiades and carry on the Silva Corporation."

I smiled at my familiar and listened to the laughter in the room. My year started out with an ugly divorce. It ended with me being one of the most powerful witches on the planet in love with a god and a house full of family and friends who would do anything to protect me. This holiday season turned out to be the best of my life despite being cursed and in danger of frying my brain.

Download the next book in the Mystical Midlife in Maine series, Saggy But Witty HERE! Then turn the page for a preview.

EXCERPT FROM SAGGY BUT WITTY IN CRESCENT CITY BOOK #5

"Are you here for more champagne?" Our resident ghost, Evanora asked as she hovered in the kitchen with us.

I loved that we had a central gathering place in the house where I could go any time of the day or night and find someone to talk to if I needed it. Typically, it was Mythia, Selene, our resident ghoul, or Evanora at four in the morning. Tonight, it was Evanora and Selene.

I rubbed my eyes as my jaw cracked on a yawn. "Not at four-fifteen in the morning. Why? Were we too loud for you last night?"

Evanora snorted. She'd picked the habit up from my sixteen-year-old daughter, Nina. "It's not like you disturbed my sleep. I'm dead, Phoebe." It was incredibly disturbing to see a ghost roll her eyes at you.

Selene set a bare rib bone down with a smile that didn't reach her eyes. Guilt washed over me for the millionth time. I still hadn't discovered a way to get her soul back inside her body like I promised. After being cursed right before Yule, having to deal with Brody's betrayal and a heart-broken

Tsekani, and having Hades over for dinner, life was still predictably chaotic. And the reason we'd extended new year's celebrations and nightly champagne for an entire week.

I walked over to her and wrapped an arm around her shoulder. "What do you say we give Fiona a call and see if she has any advice on how to put a soul in your body."

Selene brightened and gave me a big smile. "If you have time, that would be great. Don't get me wrong. I love life with you guys. However, it's weird to feel, I don't know, disconnected from everything."

My face scrunched, unable to believe what she was saying. "What exactly do you mean? And, why didn't you tell me before? I would have done something much sooner."

Evanora snorted again and drifted closer. "When? In between punishing Brody and recovering from being cursed? Your magic backed up and almost killed you less than a week and a half ago."

Selene nodded in agreement. "That's precisely why I haven't said anything. It's just getting harder to live like this. I see emotion from everyone around me and yet, the closest I came to feeling anything was the regret that consumed me after my possession."

I turned on the coffee maker, got down a mug, and a holiday blend pod. "I had no idea you were going through all that. And, you need to stop beating yourself up for that. None of it was your fault. It was the demon that took your body for a ride."

"She's right, Selene. You've been a victim two times over in some truly horrendous ways. None of what you are going through can be laid at your feet." Evanora lifted her hand like she wanted to pat Selene's shoulder and withdrew when the ghoul shivered. The ghost kept quiet during the day when everyone was around and talking over one another, so it was always surprising when she became chatty Kathy when we were alone like this.

I inserted the pod and pressed brew then grabbed my cell phone from the charger. "Thanks for backing me up, Nora. Now, let's see what Fiona has to say. She's always helped me in the past."

Selene picked up another rib. "We shouldn't wake her up this early in the morning. I don't want help that badly."

The ghoul took a big bite of the meat on the bone and chewed with a frown between her eyes. She ate all the time, making me wonder if she was trying to fill the emptiness inside. I suddenly felt so much worse. Of course, that was the reason, she didn't have a soul.

I took a sip of my coffee and coughed. I hated it black and grabbed the creamer from the fridge. "We won't be waking her up. It's nearly ten in the morning in England. She's up and going already." I added the salted caramel goodness to my java and took a hearty sip.

Selene's shoulders lowered and Evanora drifted to the corner. I motioned to the ghost with my mug. "You don't have to vanish all the time, you know. You're part of this nutty family, too."

Nora's cheeks darkened and she brushed a hand over the bonnet on her head. "I know you've said that before. It's difficult to erase centuries of behavior. It's instinct now to remain hidden or in the background."

"I understand. You do what you need to as long as you know you're one of us." I smiled at her and hit the FaceTime button for my best friend.

Fiona's smile spread across her face when she appeared on screen a second later. "Phoebe! It's good to see you even if it is o'dark thirty in Maine."

I chuckled at her reference to the ungodly hour. We got used to odd schedules working for the hospital and came up with a way to convey the time without reminding each other we weren't sleeping like we should have been.

"It's good to see you, as well. Happy belated New Years. I hope your holidays with the kids were fantastic and they took the news about their heritage with ease."

Fiona sighed and set her phone down, changing the angle of the screen. "After Bas and I rescued them from the sirens it was fabulous. Turns out Emmie nearly burned the house down and thought she was losing her mind. How were your holidays?"

I grimaced and the coffee in my mouth soured. "Aidoneus's father visited and had to help me find the witch responsible for cursing me. Tsekani was devastated to learn his boyfriend was involved. But it ended well and I think Hades might actually respect me."

Fiona shook her head. "Damn. I thought my holidays were stressful. Good to know Thanos was right about Hades. So, what can I do for you? I know you aren't calling me this early just to catch up."

I smirked at her and set my mug down. "I'm sorry. I feel like I never call unless I need something."

Fiona waved a hand through the air and smiled warmly. "The magical world is chaotic and urgent. I doubt you have time to take a relaxing bath anymore."

I laughed at her description. "You're not wrong about that. I'm calling for help with Selene, my ghoul." I turned the phone and sat next to Selene. "Have you or your Grams discovered a way to get her soul from limbo? I keep coming up empty and Aidon cannot help locate her soul. He doesn't have power over the dead. And neither does his father. Not that I would ask Hades for help. I have no desire to owe a god."

Fiona nodded her head. "Thanos has told us a little about dealing with gods and goddesses. He thinks the Dark One causing problems over here could be a pissed off goddess, but we don't have time to deal with that because we have to take Aislinn to Eidothea before her pregnancy becomes critical and kills her and her baby."

Fiona's Grams nudged her aside and put her face in the camera. "You aren't going to let her be hurt."

Fiona shrugged a shoulder. "You're right about that Grams."

I scrutinized what I could see of Fiona's Grams. "You look good, Isidora. Are you back to your normal self?"

Selene sat forward, clearly eager to hear her response. Isidora inclined her head. "I'm better than I used to be. No more aches and pains. And, I can see the fine print on labels again. My magic seems stable. I haven't used much. I prefer to spend my days writing an introductory book to the magical world. There have been far too many brought into it lately with no knowledge."

Selene set her rib down. "Do you still feel hollow inside? And crave meat?"

Isidora softened her expression as she focused on Selene. "The empty ache is gone. I no longer long for something beyond my reach, so my frustration is all but gone. However, I still eat far more meat than I ever did in my life."

Selene smiled. "That's what I needed to hear. It's getting nearly impossible to continue like this. Most of the time I want to claw my own eyes out or walk out into the ocean and let the tide take me away."

Isidora's mouth dropped open. "You cannot ever give up. I know how difficult it is, even if I didn't have to live like that as long as you."

Selene shrugged one shoulder. "I know where the zombie stories come from. I will remove myself before I snap and hurt someone I love. It seems like I have no hope, we haven't discovered a way to grab my soul from limbo and tether it to my body."

Fiona had wrapped her arm around her Grams and pulled her close. Isidora lifted a book in front of the camera. "I read something about necromancers having power over the dead. And that includes spirits and ghosts. It's not an illogical step to assume they can communicate with a soul on the other side, and possibly even bring one forth. I cannot guarantee this is the answer," Isidora warned.

Selene and I met each other and I saw the smile on my face reflected on hers. I nodded. "I get it. I should have drawn that conclusion. My only experience with them was when I killed Selene's maker."

Fiona pursed her lips. "I wouldn't have thought to seek their help, either. It makes sense. We cannot wield death magic without becoming Tainted first, so it makes sense to shy away from it."

"Do you have any idea how I can find one? I followed Selene's journey to discover her maker and somehow, I doubt I can go to our local supernatural market and ask around about one."

Isidora laughed, her blue eyes twinkling on the screen. "No, they tend to be a secretive bunch. They straddle the line between light and dark magic and make most uncomfortable. Where we deal with the energy of the earth and life, they are all about death and darkness. I recommend scrying for one under the light of the moon. It will be easier to locate one at night because that's when they're most powerful. And be sure to use water boiled with fennel, basil, clove, hibiscus, meadowsweet, orange and lavender. It stacks the odds in your favor. Grams taught me to use three black candles, as well."

I glanced out the window above the sink to our left. It was still dark outside with no sign of the impending sunrise.

We had a couple hours before the window would close. "I knew calling you guys was a good idea. I should have thought of that myself. And called you sooner, but let my pride get the best of me."

Fiona chuckled and wagged her finger. "We aren't competing for top dog in college any more. I might have been number one back them, but you are far above me now, Pheebs. Just because I know more than you, doesn't mean shit. You accidentally turned a mundie into a witch."

I shook my head from side to side. I had never viewed it as competition with Fiona. "I was never trying to be better than you, Fi. Seeing you excel pushed me to do better. It's no different now."

Fiona cocked her head to the side. "Now that you say that I see how wrong I was all those years. It never felt like you were trying to show me up or get better grades or get the promotion over me. I should have known better. I could never be close friends with someone who was jealous and competing with me."

My heart swelled and I smiled. "Never. We lift each other up. I love you, Fi. I will keep you posted about how things go. I need to get cracking on the scrying, so another supernatural crisis doesn't make me put this off again. Selene deserves to be able to leave Nimaha and have a life."

I heard Selene sniffle beside me but didn't look her way. It would make me tear up and like I told Fiona, I had some scrying to do.

Fiona held up a hand. "You know how to scry, correct? Or, do you need some assistance with that?"

"You're already familiar with the concept and I will guide you through the process. You aren't alone in this process." I was used to hearing my familiar's voice in my head and scanned the room for her. The tabby cat that I'd come to love as much as

Hattie had cared for her, walked through the archway leading to the living room.

Turning back to the phone, I shook my head. "Tarja is awake now and will be guiding me through this."

"You're lucky to have her," Isadora told me.

Fiona chuckled. "Don't accidentally search for a sexy dragon because you're bored."

It was my turn to snort. "Bored isn't something I'm familiar with. I have a sexy god to keep me occupied and paranormal problems to solve."

"We both got lucky with our new beginnings, didn't we?" Fiona mused then waved. "Let's talk soon."

"Not too soon. Text before you leave for Eidothea and call when you get back. And be careful!" My gut twisted in a knot when I thought about the danger Fiona would be in. It helped to remember she was a kickass witch that had killed an evil Fae King and Queen.

"Thanks! Love you. Bye." Fiona waved back and I tapped the red button ending the call and finished off my coffee then jumped to my feet.

"Alright. What do I need to do this thing?" I rubbed my hands together expectantly. "Do I just chant *revelare?*"

Tarja flicked her tail as she looked up at me. *"You need a silver bowl, distilled water and candles. Black ones to connect with death magic."*

Selene was up and, in the cupboard, where Mythia kept the silver dishes. I grabbed four black candles and a bottle of water from the pantry. My heart started racing and a smile grew across my face. I loved trying out new skills. Of course, everything magical was still new to me.

Tarja looked over her shoulder from the back door. I shivered looking out at the snow on the ground. This was going to be cold. I set my supplies down and grabbed my winter jacket from the laundry room and stuffed my feet into the boots I kept in there.

The cold wind sliced through me the second I opened the door like a heat seeking missile. Selene, on the other hand, didn't seem bothered as she walked out in nothing more than her jeans and sweater combo. She didn't even have shoes on. Evanora floated out beside her and went from having a bluish tinge to being white.

"It will work best if you cast the spell where the moon is shining down on you." Tarja didn't move far from the house. The door might be closed but the building shielded some of the wind. *"Focus you intent as you cast your spell."*

I took a deep breath and trudged through the snow to the middle of the yard and set the candles down. Selene handed me the bowl and backed away. I knelt down and poured the water into the vessel then turned to the candles.

"Incendo." Once all the candles around me were lit, I closed my eyes and cleared my mind. It took a few seconds to wipe all thoughts except my desire to locate a necromancer. I kept wondering about the bad side of death magic.

Keeping my need to find a necromancer at the fore, I opened my eyes and chanted the spell while keeping my gaze focused on the water in the bowl. I was thrown back when a black ghost surged out of the water.

Selene screamed as my shoulders landed on the frozen ground. I scrambled to my feet to come face to face with a black skeletal ghost covered in tattered black robes with sharp grey fangs. The smell of black licorice filled the air at the same time all will to fight fled from me.

I no longer felt like I could do anything. My life was nothing but one giant nightmare. I could barely turn my head as the ghost monster drifted toward Evanora and Selene. When they split apart and Nora tried to go through the window, the thing latched onto her leg thus stopping her escape.

Tarja hissed and jumped onto the ghost, sinking her claws in deep. *"Return the nightmare to her realm. Now."*

I gaped at my familiar. "What?" The nightmare, as she called it turned to face me and my energy drained once again.

"Reverto!" Tarja's voice bolstered me and I shouted right after her. Evanora fell into the house when the nightmare disappeared and I sucked in a full breath, glad to have the heaviness gone.

"What did I do?"

Tarja leaped from the patio to me and I caught her in my arms. My heart slowed and I calmed with her closeness. *"You called the nightmare that feeds on death forth. You were too focused on your questions. Curiosity very nearly killed the cat. This time focus on what you are looking for and nothing else."*

"Sorry," I said to Tarja and Nora. I ran a hand down my familiar's soft fur and stroked her back.

The only thought I gave any band width to was finding a necromancer. I waited a few seconds to ensure it was the only thing I wanted at the moment then cast the spell again. Tarja's energy joined mine and I felt the jolt of electricity as it activated.

Clouds replaced the glow of the moon on the water in the bowl. It reminded me a bit of the scene in one of the Harry Potter movies where Dumbledore has him view memories through his Pensieve.

The clouds cleared and the image of a mask and beads floated to the top before one of a building with a second story balcony made of metal with ornate scroll work in the corners replaced it.

I met Tarja's green eyes. "New Orleans?"

Tarja nodded. *"Yes. The city is steeped in magic. And has the biggest population of ghost in the world. Much like you, I should have known this would be the case. Gather the supplies and carry me back inside. It's freezing out here."*

I chuckled as Selene joined me and grabbed the bowl and candles for me. "We're going to New Orleans?"

I stood up and cuddle Tarja close as we walked the few feet to the back door. "Looks like it. Are you alright? You seem worried. Do you have history in the city?"

Selene shook her head as I stomped my feet clear of snow and entered the house. "No. I've always wanted to go there. It's the thought of leaving the house. I'm terrified of encountering another demon and being used to kill innocent people."

I put Tarja on the ground after I shut the door. "I know it's scary, but Aidoneus promised to help, so he will be there if the worst happens. We can't leave you like this. You should be allowed to leave the house if you want. Not be stuck here behind wards that keep you a prisoner as much as they keep you safe."

Selene's smile didn't reach her eyes. The sight reminded me of the defeated ghoul that had shown up on my doorstep a few months ago. Selene had been killed and brought back by a necromancer for some twisted purpose. We never got to discover what that purpose was because I killed the necromancer in self-defense.

"We have to prepare for the trip. Phoebe and I will continue to do research on ways we can help protect you, as well," Tarja promised.

"You know Stella will want to go with us, too. We will all be there with you." I gave her my most optimistic smile and Selene visibly relaxed. Meanwhile, I was practically shaking as I crossed mental fingers. I was in uncharted territory per usual and had no idea how I was going to navigate what I assumed would be rough waters.

AUTHORS' NOTE

Review are like hugs. Sometimes awkward. Always welcome! It would mean the world to me if you can take five minutes and let others know how much you enjoyed my work.

Don't forget to visit my website: www.brendatrim.com and sign up for my newsletter, which is jam-packed with exciting news and monthly giveaways. Also, be sure to visit and like my Facebook page https://www.facebook.com/AuthorBrendaTrim to see my daily posts.

Never allow waiting to become a habit. Live your dreams and take risks. Life is happening now.
DREAM BIG!
XOXO,
Brenda

ALSO BY BRENDA TRIM

The Dark Warrior Alliance
Dream Warrior (Dark Warrior Alliance, Book 1)
Mystik Warrior (Dark Warrior Alliance, Book 2)
Pema's Storm (Dark Warrior Alliance, Book 3)
Isis' Betrayal (Dark Warrior Alliance, Book 4)
Deviant Warrior (Dark Warrior Alliance, Book 5)
Suvi's Revenge (Dark Warrior Alliance, Book 6)
Mistletoe & Mayhem (Dark Warrior Alliance, Novella)
Scarred Warrior (Dark Warrior Alliance, Book 7)
Heat in the Bayou (Dark Warrior Alliance, Novella, Book 7.5)
Hellbound Warrior (Dark Warrior Alliance, Book 8)
Isobel (Dark Warrior Alliance, Book 9)
Rogue Warrior (Dark Warrior Alliance, Book 10)
Shattered Warrior (Dark Warrior Alliance, Book 11)
King of Khoth (Dark Warrior Alliance, Book 12)
Ice Warrior (Dark Warrior Alliance, Book 13)
Fire Warrior (Dark Warrior Alliance, Book 14)
Ramiel (Dark Warrior Alliance, Book 15)
Rivaled Warrior (Dark Warrior Alliance, Book 16)
Dragon Knight of Khoth (Dark Warrior Alliance, Book 17)
Ayil (Dark Warrior Alliance, Book 18)
Guild Master (Dark Alliance Book 19)
Maven Warrior (Dark Alliance Book 20)
Sentinel of Khoth (Dark Alliance Book 21)

Araton (Dark Warrior Alliance Book 22)

Cambion Lord (Dark Warrior Alliance Book 23)

Omega (Dark Warrior Alliance Book 24)

Dark Warrior Alliance Boxsets:

Dark Warrior Alliance Boxset Books 1-4

Dark Warrior Alliance Boxset Books 5-8

Dark Warrior Alliance Boxset Books 9-12

Dark Warrior Alliance Boxset Books 13-16

Dark Warrior Alliance Boxset Books 17-20

Hollow Rock Shifters:

Captivity, Hollow Rock Shifters Book 1

Safe Haven, Hollow Rock Shifters Book 2

Alpha, Hollow Rock Shifters Book 3

Ravin, Hollow Rock Shifters Book 4

Impeached, Hollow Rock Shifters Book 5

Anarchy, Hollow Rock Shifters Book 6

Midlife Witchery:

<u>Magical New Beginnings Book 1</u>

Mind Over Magical Matters

Magical Twist

My Magical Life to Live

Forged in Magical Fire

Like a Fine Magical Wine

Mystical Midlife in Maine

Magical Makeover

Laugh Lines & Lost Things

Hellmouths & Hot Flashes

Bramble's Edge Academy:

Unearthing the Fae King

Masking the Fae King

Revealing the Fae King

Midnight Doms:

Her Vampire Bad Boy

Her Vampire Suspect

All Souls Night

Made in the USA
Las Vegas, NV
09 October 2024

96554685R00073